Also by Mikołaj Grynberg

Survivors of the 20th Century
I Accuse Auschwitz
The Book of Exodus
I'd Like to Say Sorry, but There's No One to Say Sorry To
Jesus Died in Poland

CONFIDENTIAL

A Novel

MIKOŁAJ GRYNBERG

Translated from the Polish by Sean Gasper Bye

THE
NEW
PRESS

NEW YORK
LONDON

This publication has been supported by the ©POLAND Translation Program

Requests for permission to reproduce selections from this book should
be made through our website: https://thenewpress.com/contact.

Published in the United States by The New Press, New York, 2025
Distributed by Two Rivers Distribution

ISBN 978-1-62097-880-1 (hc)
ISBN 978-1-62097-890-0 (ebook)
CIP data is available

The New Press publishes books that promote and enrich public discussion
and understanding of the issues vital to our democracy and to a more
equitable world. These books are made possible by the enthusiasm of
our readers; the support of a committed group of donors, large and
small; the collaboration of our many partners in the independent
media and the not-for-profit sector; booksellers, who often hand-
sell New Press books; librarians; and above all by our authors.

www.thenewpress.com

Composition by Dix Digital Prepress and Design
This book was set in Centaur MT

Printed in the United States of America

2 4 6 8 10 9 7 5 3 1

If I have a smoke, I'm shot,
If I have a shot, I'm smoked.
—Zygmunt Grynberg

Contents

CONTENTS

CONFIDENTIAL

The Cacophony of the Past

Unless you know how to outrun events and, cursing the past, write a happy ending. You don't, I can tell. You got stuck, your feet are tangled in dry roots. A drought does you no good, what you could really use are months of downpours; that would make the roots slippery, you'd pull yourself out faster. Meanwhile I suggest you practice saying goodbye to your memories. For years you've been running behind, you've got to get a handle on linear time. Being locked in a memory loop is the preserve of old men, who've been cut off from retrospection by the passage of years. It's time to set time free. Take it slow, your system plays tricks on you, abrupt changes could send it into shock. Trade the circle for a timeline, not a segment—I'm sounding like some weird geometry problem.

I can't promise that, when time finally moves forward, your life will be rosy. Everything has downsides, and not many upsides. Pull your head out of the cacophony of the past. It's where you're from, but nobody's left there except you. Look around and throw out the things your children won't want to inherit. Do the same in your mind, even though that's much harder. What you can do is tell the story in lamentations. That sometimes works, it lets you put a subject at a safe distance. Safe, as in a distance that gives you a wider perspective to think about your own life. Is that something you've ever reflected on? Whether you're living well? Whose life you're living? It doesn't matter now if they'd be proud of you, that's over. Think about tomorrow, starting today.

Englishmen

Now they were just about there, they just had to leave the square and walk two hundred meters.

"If he starts screaming at the whole street again, you all go on your own this time," she said.

Ever since the boys were born, Sunday lunches at her in-laws had become mandatory. Not every week, luckily, but at least once a month. It was always the same script, one hundred percent.

They emerged from around the street corner and glanced at that same spot—the balcony on the third floor. He'd be standing there waiting, even though it was just a quarter to two. They could see him from far off, a red-haired older gentleman gesticulating energetically. The closer they got, the more clearly they could hear he wasn't restricting himself to just wildly waving his arms.

"How goddamned old are you?! Can't you stick to a schedule?! I've been standing here for fifteen minutes scared to death that something had happened to you! How dare you put my nerves through this?!"

"I meant what I said, I can't take this anymore."

"Come on, Mom, don't let it get to you. This is just how Grandpa is."

She glanced at her husband. He shrugged helplessly and gave a kind smile, raising his bushy eyebrows. She didn't want to seem hysterical, but she got fed up long ago with these balcony scenes.

"He's acting like a lunatic. Maybe this time you'll actually say something to him?" she asked, though she knew the answer full well.

"What can I say? He's telling the truth, he's scared to death and there's nothing we can do about it. Let's agree that once he dies, we'll stop visiting him." He looked at her with a warm smile.

"You think Grandpa's going to die today?" asked one of their sons.

"Hopefully not yet."

"What about you, Mom? Would you like Grandpa to die today?"

"I'd rather he didn't. We're in for plenty of excitement as it is."

Ignoring the increasingly noisy shouts coming from the balcony, they reached the stairwell, passed the mailboxes and went up the stairs. They never took the elevator; it was so tiny that there was no way all four could fit inside.

Grandpa was waiting in the open door. First he bent down to his older grandson and hugged him tight and a little too long.

"My firstborn, my firstborn. Let me see you. Boy, you sure look smart. Who'd have thought you'd be born at all!"

Next came the younger one's turn. He hugged him too tight as well.

"You've got a mop of black hair, maybe it'll lighten up. Good thing you're not a redhead."

Without taking his eyes off the boys, he hugged his son, and finally greeted his daughter-in-law, saying:

"You've given me beautiful grandsons. Come in, all of you."

"Dad, next time could you spare us the screaming from the balcony? We were supposed to come at two, we were fifteen minutes early, and you're terrified we're late?"

"It'll all be fine, don't worry. I was worried you'd gotten hit by a car or some other disaster . . . The most important thing is we're all alive and we're together. Incidentally, I wonder how many great-grandsons I'll get to see. Well boys, can I count on you?"

"I don't know if you'll live long enough," said the younger grandson.

"Look, what a joker!" Grandpa laughed and grinned.

After the greetings, they went through to the dining room, which held a large round table. The white tablecloth, gold-edged plates and silver cutlery—everything was already prepared. Sitting at the table was an old woman, tiny and hunched. For years she'd been suffering from Alzheimer's, and she didn't react to the noise that filled the room.

"Boys, say hello to Grandma," said Father.

They didn't like getting close to her, they didn't understand what was wrong with her. They rarely heard her speak, and when she did, it was hardly ever in Polish. They went up to her, quickly kissed her on the cheek and sat down in their places. Sometimes a barely noticeable smile flickered across her wrinkled face, whether consciously or not, it was hard to say.

Grandpa's housekeeper had cooked lunch. She placed the pots and pans on the windowsill and left, despite sincere invitations to join everyone at the table. Homemade chicken noodle soup, ground cutlets, mashed potatoes, and lettuce with sweet cream, which no one ate except Grandpa. The younger grandson quickly wolfed down his whole meal so he could get seconds of the soup before it disappeared back into the kitchen. Later he politely asked to be excused from the table and sat down on the floor, where he played with his toy cars.

The rhythm of their lunches was unchanging. It all lasted about an hour and a half, then Grandpa would catch forty winks and they, with no one to stop them, would leave.

"Did you hear the one about the bodybuilder from Dachau? He picked up a brick and then he was pooped!"

"Oh God!" wailed Grandma in Polish.

Silence fell, and the parents' eyes turned toward their elder son.

"He didn't learn that from me!"

"My friends at school taught it to me," said the youngest member of the family, without an ounce of embarrassment.

"Why did you decide to share it with us at this very moment?" asked Father.

"I just remembered it."

"Look at him, he just remembered it! And did you know that some people have never been able to forget?" asked Grandpa, enraged.

"Yeah."

"And how, may I ask?"

"From you guys, you keep talking about it. I don't get why you're always going on about Jews."

"Because we are Jews," replied Grandpa.

"All of us?"

Grandpa looked around and smiled.

"Yes, all of us."

"Me too?"

"You too."

The boy returned for a moment to his toy cars.

"I'd rather be an Englishman," he said after a long silence.

"Can I tell you something?" asked Grandpa.

"Sure."

"I'd rather be an Englishman too."

Grandpa reached for his glass of tea, but by then it had gone so cold he lost interest. He got up from the table and went to take a nap.

I Tell Everybody

The guy was the joking type. He loved medical science and women, in that order. Meanwhile half the city loved him—the half he treated. The second half was divided into those he infuriated and those who were indifferent. He was redheaded and freckled, in other words, temperamental. He was capable of unexpectedly punching someone in the face, necking a half-liter of vodka, and moving on as if nothing had happened.

He'd made it into the second half of the twentieth century and resolved to make the most of the opportunity by living without renouncing pleasure. He figured he'd had his fill of tragedies. His wife saw to raising their child, and he got involved only when the situation called for a doctor. He saw a father's lot as a thankless one, like in the joke about the son who's a picky eater. The whole family's concerned, he's skinny, he's not eating anything. Finally the father can't take it anymore and asks what his son would like most. The kid thinks a little and says, shit. What do you mean shit?

Like I said, shit. Shit on a plate. Mother looks at father, father at mother, then he gets up and goes to the bathroom. He comes back with shit on a plate. He sets it in front of his son. The boy examines it and says he wants fried shit. Mother looks at father, father at mother, then he gets up and goes to the kitchen. He comes back and sets it in front of his son. The son examines it and says he wants Dad to try it. Mother at father, father at mother. He tries it, says it's delicious, and encourages his son to finally start eating. Nah, he says, you already ate the best part.

The household hummed along, their son grew like a beanstalk, and the red-haired doctor met woman after woman and had moments of passion with them. When friends asked how he was doing, he'd tell the joke about the Jew who comes to a priest to confess. The priest asks if the penitent is Catholic. He isn't. So why has he come? Because he really needs to. The priest goes into the confessional and the Jew starts telling him about all the women he's recently slept with. How this one was blonde, that one had curly hair, and yet another had these small breasts . . . Why did you pick me of all people to tell this to? asks the priest. The Jew says, I tell everybody.

• • •

His wife kept pretending not to hear. After what they'd been through, she knew there were more serious problems life could bring. Sometimes she complained to her best friend, who when she got home would ask her husband to have a word with the doctor. The two men would make plans to get a vodka together, and the family friend would delicately reveal the mission he'd been sent with. The redhead would peer at him and say he just remembered the joke about the tax collector who comes to see the Jewish community. What do you do with the wax from the melted candles? We gather it up and make it into new candles. I see. And what do you do with the crumbs from the matzo? Oh, we use them to make delicious matzo balls. I see. And when you circumcise little boys, what do you do with the, well, you know? Ah, those. We gather them up, we send them to the tax office, and they send us dicks like you.

The doctor would shut down the friendly overtures in the blink of an eye. If his interlocutor was persistent, he'd call a waitress over and ask her to open a window. Nothing to fear, he'd say, my friend's not a bee, he won't buzz off.

His son married a young woman with black hair, a graduate of the Academy of Fine Arts. The doctor had in fact had other plans for him, but the old man got the message and stopped hunting for an ideal match.

The wife of the redheaded doctor began suffering from aggressive Alzheimer's. He took perfect care of her. He brought a young girl from the provinces into the house. She cooked, took care of the sick wife, and got very cozy with the doctor too.

To his grandsons he became a wonderful doctor and an odd grandpa, who periodically had flights of fancy. Once a year he took them shopping. He could surprise everybody by buying a billiard table or a bicycle. Sometimes he'd take them to a restaurant, and after ordering he'd quickly vanish. Years later, as his grandsons grew up, they realized that his slipping off wasn't at all about ditching them, it was because of a waitress in a short skirt. He didn't know how to be a grandfather, yet he was proud that his family was growing.

A year after his wife died, he took his older grandson out to lunch. After placing their orders, he didn't leave the table as usual. While they waited for their food, Grandpa remembered the joke about Rosenzweig, who's pacing around the house all night long. At about five in the morning, his wife gets up, furious, and asks what he keeps pacing like that for. I'm pacing because I can't sleep, replies Rosenzweig. Why can't you sleep? Because I owe money to Hozenduft. A lot? A lot. So call him and tell him you won't pay. The husband thinks for a moment and phones. This is Rosenzweig. Yes, I know what time it is. I just wanted to say I won't pay you that money back, goodnight. And he hangs up. So what now? he asks his wife. Go to bed, she says, now he's the one who can't sleep.

The grandson, although he's been trained in the art of

the joke since childhood, can't understand why Grandpa's telling this one at this particular moment. A shapely waitress brings their food. Grandpa smiles at her, but stays at the table.

"Listen, there's this Jewish law that says a healthy man shouldn't be on his own. The law also says that when a wife dies, her husband can marry her sister. Your grandma's sister died back when everyone did."

What now? thinks the grandson. His grandfather takes a deep breath and informs him he's getting married. He immediately adds that his son isn't going to be happy with his choice of a wife.

"How do you know?" asks the grandson.

"I've got a feeling. It's rare to like your stepmother. My stepsister couldn't stand my mother."

"Did she have reasons?" asks the grandson.

"Oh, she had nothing but reasons!"

The grandson worries he's been deputized to report this strange news to his father. He can sense it will be neither easy nor pleasant. Salvation comes unexpectedly.

"But let's not tell your father anything for now . . ." his grandfather tells him, then pauses. "A second wife, one for your old age, you choose without thinking about other people. You look for someone who'll understand you. Even if you know she speaks before she thinks, that she's difficult, that she'll hurt everyone all around. You get into it because you want to drown out the loneliness. You think that later on you can deal with her not fitting in."

His grandson is a teenager and has the feeling that later on might be too late, but this is grownups' business, after all. He doesn't yet know that in his family, this type of stepmother will turn out to be hereditary.

The Neptune Factor

Lies don't have short legs. His father always said they did, but he didn't know how wrong he was. They'll make their way to the surface when you're not alert enough to keep them hidden.

When he was little, he didn't lie—they said he made up beautiful stories. By the time he was a teenager, they called it lying. He didn't give it much thought and tailored his life to suit himself.

He was forging a system of values to meet the needs of the moment.

The most important principle: peaceful parents—peaceful life. This system had some holes, but in time it became an integral part of a cycle: to ensure his parents peace between parent-teacher conferences, and to survive their return from parent-teacher conferences with dignity and with hope for a better tomorrow. To find solace in the house's post-argument calm and not to take grievances or anger personally. After a few days, to give them something to lift their spirits, which didn't have to be true or important to work for the time being. To remember that the principle of "peaceful parents— peaceful life" was the priority, and that the best moments came between parent-teacher conferences. Not to be reckless, but also not to surrender by default.

He was cheerful, the first postwar child in his family. He could sense that they struggled to tolerate unreliability. He crafted a naturalistic modus operandi. You could say he took his model from nature itself. He moved the way a stream flows—where there was the least resistance, rather than where was expected. A principle as simple as it was disapproved of.

The door opened and a streak of light fell into the movie theater.

"Anyone here by the name of . . . ?" and then his last name.

He thought he'd misheard.

"Anyone here by the name of . . . ?"

Now he had no doubt. Nor—unfortunately—did the girl he'd invited to the movies.

"His full name, please come to the exit. Your mom is waiting at the box office."

He was thirteen years old and 145 centimeters tall. He squeezed down into the theater seat, but he could already sense that this semester, the house would get into parent-teacher conference mood well in advance. He didn't dare glance at the first girl he'd ever invited to the movies.

"His first name and last name, please get up and come to the exit, or else I'll turn on the lights."

There was no chance of escape, the usher was standing in one door and his mother in the other. And he'd been doing so well with this girl! He'd talked her into slipping out of afterschool club together, which wasn't easy. He'd stolen the money for tickets from his mother, which had also called for a trace of cunning. He'd just been starting to consider slowly lifting his arm and placing it on the backrest right behind his classmate. Everything had been going according to the plan arising fluidly in his teenage mind. Midway through the screening of *The Neptune Factor* he felt like he was growing up. With the hostile light from the theater hallway, his plans fell into ruin. He was overcome with rage. He got up, leaned over to the girl's ear and said:

"I'm sorry, I'll see you tomorrow."

"You couldn't let me finish watching?" he attacked.

He was still too young to know that this strategy wouldn't work.

"And did you forget that I was supposed to pick you up early? We have a doctor's appointment."

He had forgotten. Ever since his friend agreed to go to the movies with him, he couldn't remember a thing. Classes had let out an hour beforehand and the two of them were sitting in afterschool club, disgustedly watching the afterschool supervisor, who'd pulled off her stockings and was clipping her toenails. She did this from time to time. Then she'd pick one of the girls to sweep the clippings off the floor.

Now or never. They'd risen from their chairs and slowly crept to the door. The teacher was sitting sideways and still clipping her toenails. He turned the handle, opened the door, let his classmate out first, and in absolute silence they both left.

As they were running to the movie theater, a block away from their school, he felt like he was soaring. It was the start of the school year, his life looked rosy. They were running side by side, as if it were summer and they were already over eighteen. She was smiling, her braid floating like the tail of a kite, her breasts bouncing rhythmically.

"How did you know where to look for me?"

"First I'd like to know where you got money for the ticket."

"Tickets."

"Who did you go with?"

"Someone important, you've spoiled everything."

The doctor told his mother not to worry, her son was short now, but he had big feet, which meant he'd grow into a strapping lad.

When they got home he went straight to bed, pulling the comforter over his head.

"Get up, coward!" shouted his father, turning on the lights in the room.

The boy knew what would happen, because it happened after every parent-teacher conference. He knew how the evening would run, including the words his younger brother would say when the boy came back to their shared room after the talk with their parents.

"You're not going to do that again, right? You get that lies always have short legs?" his brother asked, in his father's words.

He did get it, which didn't mean he agreed. While his brother appreciated peace and quiet, to him, moments of freedom brought a joy that far outweighed the unpleasantness of a parental reprimand.

The next day—not without fear—he went to school, and his classmate wasn't there. Nor did she come the next day, nor the day after that. She and her parents had emigrated to Sweden. But hadn't he told her, "I'm sorry, I'll see you tomorrow"? He felt something had slipped through his fingers that he didn't yet know how to name.

• • •

Twenty years later he read a short story by a Swedish writer called "The Neptune Factor." About two young people in love, hiding from the world in a movie theater. About the best moment in her life.

Yearsatears

She grew up in houses that weren't homes. Well, maybe except for the first one, but only in comparison with what life would later bring. For her first year she had both parents, and in her second one they were still alive, which in those days was a pretty good result.

As the first baby in her parents' group of friends, she was enveloped in love, attention, and misplaced faith in the future. In her second year, she no longer saw her father, which didn't mean he no longer saw her. Mama would take her to the Parc des Buttes Chaumont in Paris, so her father could look at her. Mama would sit on a bench with the baby carriage on the edge of the path, right by the bushes. She turned it around so the baby would face where her papa was hidden. This went on for a few months, until the bushes became empty. The leaves were gone, and her hidden father was too. The French state railroad had shipped him to where people like him from all over Europe were shipped off to. At that time, she didn't yet know what it meant to miss a balding face with glasses, poking out of the urban greenery.

When she was three, the concierge came into the apartment and took her home with her. She was glad, because for many hours she'd been waiting for her mama. She'd been waiting longer than usual, and in those days that was a much worse sign than it is today.

For a while she lived with the concierge, who was very glad when someone finally took away this girl who kept repeating again and again: "Où est ma maman?"

This new place, full of children, was not what she'd been dreaming of. She'd never gone to daycare or preschool. She'd only ever had one friend before, whose mother also took her on walks in Buttes Chaumont. She wanted to snuggle up to her beautiful mama and lie in bed with her, and she wouldn't even mind her mother squeezing her tight and crying.

In the orphanage she slept alone, most of the children cried all night, and her mama wasn't there. She spent just enough time in the first orphanage to stop crying every night. Then a couple arrived who said they were friends of her mama's, and without giving her time to say goodbye to the other children, they took her home with them. She got a bed in a room that a boy lived in. He was nice, and for the rest of her life she called him "mon frère de lait." Now she knew how not to cry, but in the new place it didn't always work. Once she'd forgotten slightly about crying, it turned out she needed to move on. This time she got to say goodbye both to the boy and to his parents. She had really grown to like them.

A woman she had never seen before brought her a red lollipop. The woman spoke French strangely, interspersed every now and then with Polish words. She liked listening to her, because the sound reminded her of the days when she lived with Mama. She found out they were taking a long journey on a train. The woman said to call her "maman" and promised her another lollipop once they arrived.

The journey took all day. The new lady only got annoyed when the girl said: "Maman, où est ma maman?" They arrived at a place where even in the evening it was very warm. She quickly realized she was back in an orphanage. She wasn't happy, but now she knew how to behave. She got another lollipop. When they said goodbye, the woman looked ready to burst into tears. Luckily she didn't. It was at this orphanage that she made the most friends. She often told stories about the boy whose mama came to visit him twice. He had a turtle that he never parted with.

When the adults were jumping for joy that the war was over, she was living in yet another orphanage. It wasn't bad there at all. She didn't cry, but in sad moments she'd cuddle the younger children. She didn't know what the end of the war would bring, but she could see it made the grownups ecstatic.

Now everyone was used to peace, but still nothing changed.

Just as she was helping the younger children wash their hands before lunch, two figures paused in the door to the bathroom: a housemistress and a witch. They waited until the little ones had gone to the cafeteria, then very slowly approached her. The witch was almost bald, she had no teeth, and her hands were shaking hard.

"I'm your mama."

"My mama was beautiful, she had teeth and thick hair."

The witch's eyes filled with tears.

By the time she'd joined the other children at the table, she wasn't thinking about her mama.

The next day the witch came again. Then another time. After the fourth visit she kept trying to remember her mama, but she could only recall teeth and hair. On the fifth visit she shouted: "Va-t'en !" and watched with satisfaction as this pseudomama left in tears. On the sixth day her mama brought chocolate. On the seventh day they ate it together and went home.

She slept in bed with her mama, ate with her mama, washed with her mama, went on walks in the park with her mama. Mama would cry so hard that they once had to sit down on a bench. She herself didn't know how to cry, so that was the only thing they didn't do together.

They moved in with a friend of Mama's, who was very

skinny and sometimes sad. He gathered up all of Mama for himself. She went to school, where many children had a mama and a papa. She came home and asked: "Où est mon papa?" Mama started crying and said he was gone now.

"But he used to be here?" she asked.

"He did."

"So maybe he'll come back?"

Mama cried harder and harder. It looked as though the conversation was over.

From time to time she tried to bring it up again, but without success.

"Do you know where my papa is?" she asked her mama's friend.

He said he didn't know, but later it turned out he was lying, because he did.

She was seven and repeated first grade, this time in Poland. She didn't know the language, but she met two friends from the orphanage who didn't speak Polish either. One of them was the boy with the turtle. They stuck together and didn't talk about where they'd met.

She wasn't always brave enough at school to ask the meaning of words she didn't yet know. Usually she'd only ask once she got home.

"What are 'yearsatears'?"

"What?"

"Yearsatears."

"There's no such word in Polish. Where did you hear it?"

"For the battle, for the blood, for the yearsatears. It's this song we sing every day."

It soon turned out she had a new last name. Not one like in France. Now she shared a name with the man who lied that he didn't know what happened to her papa.

"Done! I got a driver's license and got her last name changed," he said one day, as soon as he walked in the door.

Passover

They grew up in a house that smelled like home. You just had to enter the little hallway to catch its scent, which was unlike any other house they knew. You could smell it best after returning from vacation, concentrated, but not musty or heavy, not evoking neglect. If you were to break it down into prime factors, you would have coffee, toast, Mom's perfumes, and Dad's drawer full of pipes and napkins with brown coffee stains. A more expert nose would also detect a whiff of liqueurs homemade from unpitted sour cherries, the rusting blades of a few wooden-handled French knives, and amid them, the barely perceptible scent of lavender from the linen shelf.

They were both long since grown up, they had wives and children. They spent a lot of time at headquarters—as their friends referred to the house. Sometimes for lunches together, and sometimes without notice, to drink coffee and chat.

Recently the house had been enriched by a new scent. A trifle flowery, light, but not evocative of youth.

Grandma—Mom's mom—had moved into their parents' old room. After her husband died they'd persuaded her to move in. Their parents took over their sons' old room. The apartment was once again a home for two generations.

Mom phoned her sons and asked them to come over, without their families this time. They were surprised, and above all concerned. They arrived before noon; only Mom and Grandma were home.

"It's good you're here. Don't worry, I'm not dying. Have a seat, I'll just ask Grandma to give us a moment to talk."

"We'll go say hello to Grandma."

"I think she's dozing after breakfast, hold on a second."

The brothers sat down side by side at the oak kitchen table where they'd spent their whole childhoods. Before them lay a paper folder of documents.

"Who's here?" asked Grandma from her room.

"I'm coming, Mama!" shouted Mom and she left the kitchen.

One of the brothers wanted to take a look at the papers, but the second firmly resolved they would wait until Mom showed what they were.

"Don't you wonder what's inside?"

"Try to be patient for once."

Mom disappeared for a short while inside Grandma's room, then poked her head out through the door.

"Come say hello."

Grandma was sitting in an armchair, wearing a bathrobe.

"Who do I see? You don't usually come at this time. Did something happen?"

They didn't know themselves what had happened, so they said it was nothing, gave her their greetings and went straight back into the kitchen to wait for mom.

"Boys, I've caused you a little trouble, but I needed to, I had no choice."

"Can you be more specific?" asked one, on behalf of them both.

Ever since their teenage arguments had ended, neither son had been summoned by their parents to talk. Their minds were a mix of anxiety and curiosity. Up until now one of them had been the specialist in causing trouble. It looked like he'd lost his monopoly.

"For fifty years I've dreamed of having Dad's last name, and I've finally done it."

"You have got Dad's last name."

"I mean my Dad."

"You changed your name?" they asked simultaneously.

"I changed my maiden name. Now I'm going to have the

same name I had for the first six years of my life. I'll be my father's daughter again."

A shout came from Grandma's room.

"Coming, Mama!"

Their mom went to her mom.

"Do you see how this is supposed to cause us problems?" one brother asked the other.

"I don't, but we're about to find out."

"Give me a second, boys. I have to bring Grandma some coffee, I'll be right back," she said as she walked into the kitchen.

"Ever since I found out my dad was murdered and the name I have isn't his, I've felt like I was treating him unfairly. I've waited a really long time. Too long. The longer I waited, the worse I felt about it."

"For days now my daughter won't talk about anything other than the Jews' imprisonment in Egypt," said one of the sons.

"Can you be serious for a moment?" asked the other.

"I was worried you'd be mad." Mom smiled.

"That you've come out of bondage?" asked the father of the daughter recently preoccupied with Egyptian slavery.

"That you'd think it was silly."

"Why didn't you do it earlier?"

"I didn't want to offend my stepfather."

"Are the boys still here?" asked Grandma from her room.

"Yes," replied Mom.

"I'll come out in a second, will you help me get dressed?" Grandma wasn't giving in.

"In a second, Mama."

"Have you told Grandma?"

"No, and I don't think I will, because it doesn't make any difference at all to her."

"How do you know? Maybe she'll be glad. I'm sure she'd be proud of you."

"I'm leaving that for later. If I told her I was going back to Dad's name, I'd have to tell her how I felt when she took me out of the orphanage, and how I hated her for giving all her attention to her new husband and leaving nothing for me."

"You've never talked about that?"

"Never."

"Maybe now's the time."

"After that conversation, I don't think we could live together anymore."

"I would try."

"Can't you hear what Mom's saying?" said the more rational of the brothers.

"Let's get back to what this means for you," replied Mom, blowing her nose and wiping her eyes. "Now you're going to have to update a lot of documents. From me you'll get new birth certificates, but the rest you'll have to sort out your-selves. I'm sorry for the trouble."

"It's no trouble. Were you afraid we wouldn't understand?"

"I've been thinking about this for so many years I was afraid of everything."

"You never talked about it."

"I didn't know how."

"I don't know anyone who's changed their maiden name."

"A lot of people are going back to their real names as adults. Even in Poland."

"Seems like that includes us now. Do new birth certificates mean that all the other documents we have are invalid?" asked one of the brothers with amusement.

"Yes," replied Mom with a slight smile.

"Schools, universities, marriage certificates, our children's birth certificates . . . ? "

"I think so. Now I feel like it's really happened."

"Are you coming or am I supposed to drag myself out there?" shouted Grandma impatiently.

"We're coming!"

On Sunday, both brothers and their families arrived at head-quarters for lunch.

"Grandma, you have no idea how glad I am that you're also interested in the exodus of the Jews from Egypt," said the seven-year-old girl.

The more rational brother looked at the other and shook his head at his foolishness.

After the Lesson

"If I can't trust you, who can I trust?" asked Father.

It was early spring, but everything around suggested it was still the middle of winter. Frozen snow lay on the sidewalks, gray with age. Though the sun wasn't meant to set for another hour, it was already nearly dark. The sky hung four stories above the ground and faithfully imitated the color of the snow.

He was twelve and had just finished a French lesson. He walked out to the parking lot in front of his tutor's apartment building, where his father was meant to be waiting. His parents counted on him being self-reliant, but now and then someone would pick him up so he didn't have to come back through city alone in the dark. The bus home took forty-five minutes and meandered along the river.

"Hi," he said, getting into the car.

"Hi," replied his father.

The car didn't move, and his father looked at him wordlessly.

"If I can't trust you, who can I trust?" he said a second time.

"I don't know what you mean," he replied, perplexed.

"Where did you get this?" His father pulled from his pocket a wad of foreign currency certificates, unrolled them and lay them on his thigh. "Fifty-five cents. Where did you get these?"

He was too young to quickly think up a sentence like "I found them on the street, wrapped in newspaper."

"Where did you get these?" asked his father again.

He didn't have a good answer, so he chose silence. He knew that would not ease the situation, but he was playing for each second.

"Did you steal them from my desk drawer?"

"No."

"Then where did you get them?"

". . ."

"Is this your money?"

"No."

"So why did I find it in your drawer?"

It didn't occur to him to ask why he was searching his desk.

"Can you answer my questions?"

The trouble was he couldn't. He didn't know how to own up to the theft that his father was accusing him of. He didn't think of it in the categories his father was using. The certificates just let him go to the luxury Pewex store, where you had to pay in dollars, and buy imported candy. Tic Tacs, for instance, which gave him an incredible social boost among his friends.

"How is it possible for my son to steal?"

He couldn't bear to stay in the car. He didn't know if his father called after him, he just remembered that he ran. He fled the pressure, the feeling of guilt, and the trap he found himself in. His twelve-year-old brain didn't know how to invent answers that would let him start a negotiation. He ran through the parking lot, hopped over the low fence separating the sidewalk from the wide, divided roadway and, slipping on the asphalt, he reached the other side. He didn't turn around; he was fleeing his own shame. He wasn't certain if his father would look for him, or if he was so mad and disappointed that he'd drive off without him. Twice he crossed back and forth across the wide road, once going all the way down to the river alongside, but he quickly returned to the sidewalk.

He made his way home. He was walking slowly, to make his father worry longer. He didn't know what awaited him once he arrived. He'd stolen money from his parents a couple of other times. He'd only been caught once. He'd pinched a bill from his mother's purse and spent four-fifty on a paperback of *Four Tankmen and a Dog*. It was hard to call this the perfect crime, since he was no expert on banknotes. He'd only needed to get ten złotys, but unfortunately he took five hundred. When the seller gave him his change, he didn't know what to do with so much money, which barely fit in his little pockets. Just past his house they were constructing a new apartment complex, and there he buried everything the man in the kiosk had given him. The disappearance of one-fifth of mom's salary did not go unnoticed. The pressure was so strong that he fairly quickly decided to come clean. After two hours of searching—during which both he and his father, equipped with plastic shovels, dug up every spot he pointed out—his father gave up, resigned, and they went back home. He didn't remember being punished at all. What stayed with him was the panicked fear he felt at the sight of the mountain of money. His memories of them digging through heaps of sand together aren't so bad. His father was kind and they both tried really hard.

He reached home late that evening. Before he worked up the nerve to enter the apartment, he stood for a long time in front of the door. Before he could even get his shoes off, his mother appeared in the entryway. She burst into tears and hugged him very tight, so tight he could barely catch his breath. He didn't protest, because just a few seconds earlier he'd had no idea what kind of welcome he was in for. She was crying so hard—it was the first time he'd seen her in such a state—that her legs couldn't hold her up, and they slowly sank to the floor.

"What would you have done if he hadn't come back?" she screamed to her husband. "What would you have done?"

His father stared at them for a moment before disappearing into his room.

They sat there a while longer on the cold, red-tiled floor. His anxiety over what would happen after he returned slowly transformed into concern for his mother. It was hard to say when she was no longer the one hugging him, but he the one hugging her, as she sobbed in his arms. He knew what he and his father would soon be talking about. They'd already had several such conversations.

"You know what's wrong with mom?"

"She's feeling blue."

"Do you know what makes her feel blue?"

"Yes, but I don't know how to explain it," replied the son.

A Funeral Scenario

She goes to funerals to see other people's tears.

The chatter builds, the musicians tune their instruments, the void begins to take form, just like at the symphony before the concert starts. Funerals have their own choreography, too. First the deceased's family arrives and waits until the protagonist is brought from the funeral home. They sort things out with the gravediggers discreetly and off to one side. Small groups of acquaintances and friends link up into larger herds. No one cries yet; for now, they all communicate in glances.

Most keep a safe distance from the family of the deceased.

She never gets close. She comes to observe, not to participate.

• • •

The coffin laid out on the catafalque, the name card wobbling on its stand, and below them, a flower bed with wreaths and bouquets.

The guests laying flowers behave like an official state delegation at the Tomb of the Unknown Soldier. They squat awkwardly, place what they've brought on the cold floor, adjust their scarves, then stand at attention and, with an energetic motion, nod, hold for a moment, jerk their heads back up, take a step back, pivot and, this time with a gentle shake of their heads and a dignified closing of the eyes, turn to approach the deceased's family.

She weighs which seat to pick. To sit down right behind the family and see everything up close, even the smallest gestures of mutual support, passing one another tissues and wiping away tears, or to choose an alternative spot—worse, but not without its advantages—at the back of the room, right by the wall? A position offering a wide angle: who glances at who, who is late, who cries, who sneaks a peek at their neighbors' faces.

She awaits the climax, which comes in the eulogies by the closest family. This is the time for others' tears. She jealously drinks them from their faces.

She can remember from childhood that tickle that used to come with crying, a memory far too distant. Standing among the mourners, she does her best to trigger in herself the biological reaction that for years she has missed. At every funeral, she wagers that someone else's death will bring her momentary relief. Just a few tears, many at best, and then finally a series of convulsive gasps, the kind that rock a child just after they've stopped sobbing.

She'd been to many funerals, but at none had she shed even one tear. She didn't stop going, she didn't lose hope.

The remedy for these failures is the solitary return from the cemetery. She walks out the gate, and the same scenario starts playing in her head.

She learns that she's sick. It's always an untreatable illness, the kind that brings great pain and wrecks the body. She must live alone with this news, she carries on without burdening anyone, neither her husband nor either of her sons. She draws strength from her own bravery. The worse she feels, the prouder she is.

The time comes when she can no longer get out of bed on her own. In front of her loved ones, she plays the role of a cheerful patient who always stays positive. When she thinks of her sons, she imagines their life without her. She sees them alone, missing her and inconsolable. She knows they're sensitive, her death will come as a hard blow to them. All the harder because they don't talk about what's about to happen. She reflects on her husband's future life. She doesn't know if she'd prefer for him to be alone or to find a new partner who will make him happy. She worries whether the boys will take a liking to their stepmother and whether they'll manage to form a good family. Better if the new woman doesn't have children. Though something might be wrong with her if she doesn't. Maybe it was worth talking to her husband about it now and warning him.

The postfuneral scenario follows a well-worn track, but her eyes are still without the tears she so badly desires.

The disease progresses, she finds it harder and harder to roll over on her own. She talks to her husband mainly about how to arrange the pillows, how many there should be and at what angle. Sometimes with a smile on her face she encourages him to send her—once he's had enough— to a hospice or a nursing home. She assures him that she sees this as natural and how things should be. She doesn't want to cause trouble, lingering in the room like a pang of conscience.

She instructs them how to feed her and invents a set of signals they'll use to communicate once she stops speaking. Pain, pillows higher, pillows left, drink, eat, diaper, cold, warm, give me oxygen, radio on/off, television on/off, change channel, people can come visit you, but don't bring them to see me, get Dad, get your older son . . . It looks like they're ready for the next stage.

Their communication works flawlessly, they just talk differently now. She's proud of her children, she looks on her husband and smiles. She can no longer move at all on her own, all that's left are looking and blinking. She knew it would be this way, that's why she also created a system based on eye movements.

She lies there, and family life continues on the other side of the wall. They haven't brought her to a hospice or a nursing home. The pillows are perfectly arranged, it's not too cold, but under the middle of her back she can feel a small crease in the bedsheet that chafes more and more. She waits patiently until a member of the household looks in on her. When they do, she tries to let them know, it's chafing, her back . . . Unfortunately her set of signals has no code for that.

• • •

Tears slowly flow out from under her eyelids.

"Why are you crying again?" asks her husband as he picks her up from the funeral.

"I'm feeling blue, it'll pass soon," she replies.

It was worth going to that funeral, she thinks.

The Conditional Perfect

Who knows, maybe if not for the war, he would never have been born. What a paradox—after all, war is more about the end of life than the beginning.

They met in a retirement home, though they were both around forty—she a little over, he a little under. She was an accountant there, and he, a volunteer—treating elderly Jews.

This experienced lady-killer quickly won her over. They slept together in July, but by September war had broken out. Who knows what would have happened if peace had endured for longer, maybe they would have broken up, maybe had an abortion.

Time flew by, no one knew how long this would last. Their natural instincts brought them closer. Before they realized it, the war had made them a family.

He was born in April, and by November they were in the ghetto. As a trio.

There, people were suffering from typhus and the risk of deportation. The first was simply deadly, for the second, medicine knew no cure. They had enough savings for two people;

at dawn the three-year-old and his mother were smuggled out under a pile of dirty underwear to the safer side—insofar as, for people like them in those days, there was a safer side. Sitting under the floor in the home of good people, they counted the days. They counted up too many to be hopeful, but they found it hard to stop. When the air ceased fluttering with flakes of burned books and soot, and the stench was less palpable, the chestnut trees blossomed. Then they stopped counting.

The doctor rejoined his family when no one was waiting for him any longer.

If he hadn't found a bunker stocked with water and food in the ghetto, he wouldn't have survived. In a short time all their lives would have come to an end.

"You have to watch out, because around good people there are often bad ones lurking," he kept saying for the rest of his life.

Their good hosts got a visit from people who sold Jewish life cheaply, quickly and unhesitatingly. They moved out from under the floor; you didn't have to tell them twice.

If not for a series of glimmers of happiness, they wouldn't have lasted until the next winter, which, apart from cold, brought relief.

The boy was five years old and as lucky as it gets to have survived until liberation. While the grownups celebrated the end of the war, he kept finishing off what was left in their glasses. Rectified spirit with raspberry syrup—so-called "papa and mama"—almost killed him. If his father hadn't been a doctor, the child survivor would have perished on the first day of freedom.

Life got back on a track that's considered safe; the boy graduated from high school and went to university. His father believed to the bitter end that he'd be able to talk his son into medical school. But doctor's stories over Sunday lunch, combined with the prospect of getting up close and personal with blood, took its toll. In times when it was said the twentieth century had split the atom, what tempted an intelligent, young mind were the hard sciences.

He graduated from university and married.

They both had different anxieties. He, that he'd be hungry and cold, like in the hideout. She feared loneliness and rejection. These were the emotions she knew from the French orphanages where she'd spent the war. They were charred with the past, but youth has a strength that can lift you off the ground.

Except youth disappeared when most of their close friends were forced out of the country.

"Poland is a land that, when it wishes, is capable of sacrificing a portion of its citizens," the doctor used to say.

They knew this wasn't the first time; then they understood it definitely wouldn't be the last.

They remained with their loved ones, not going out into the wider world. The stories of their families told them they had to do everything to keep from being separated.

The neurologist said that if not for the misdiagnosis, the stroke would have destroyed him. He was diabetic, the paramedics in the ambulance had thought it was a hypoglycemic coma and pumped him full of glucose. Apparently that saved his brain.

Six months later he returned to his department, a year later he was teaching again. He'd changed a bit. He was calmer and had lost weight.

If not for the stroke, his wife probably wouldn't have gone to the country with him. He'd insisted on closing down the family summer house for the winter. He wanted to clean the rotting leaves out of the gutters. She was afraid he'd fall off the ladder, so she went to look after him.

They were driving out of the city by ten in the morning on a sunny day in late November. On the way, it started snowing.

If they hadn't had snow tires, that would have been some explanation. But they did.

If a delivery truck hadn't been driving in front of them, everything would have been fine. Unfortunately, one was. A big clump of snow popped out from under it and clogged their left front wheel. Though they were driving slowly, the car flipped onto its left side, fell into a ditch and struck a concrete culvert. The driver's airbag worked, the passenger's didn't. She hit her head on the glove compartment.

They got out of the car. He used his handkerchief to wipe the wound on her head. They were both in shock. After a while, an ambulance arrived and brought her to the hospital.

Twenty minutes later, she was unconscious, and in five days, she died.

At the end of winter, he was charged with causing a fatal accident. His guilt was so deep that he met the accusation with indifference and said he wasn't going to defend himself. His sons asked a lawyer friend of the family for help, and she spent many hours talking to him about the pointlessness of adding to the misfortune. He was stubborn, he wanted to go to prison. He'd found a form of solace.

• • •

The defense's strategy was strengthened by a letter from his children.

Your Honor,

We have had the good fortune to be raised by two wonderful people. Both of them came into life at a time when, as a rule, people like them had no right to live.

They managed to, even though all the signs around them and their family histories seemed to indicate they couldn't.

They grew up in families steamrolled by history. They were stripped of the basic feeling of safety right from the start. In the name of the law.

They made a family—something that had no right to work out. They gave us everything we deserved. To this day we don't know where they drew their strength or their role models. We know we got a good and happy childhood, that we always felt their support.

Accusing our father of killing our mother is a misunderstanding; that is not what happened on that snowy road. You do not kill someone who gives you the strength to live another day.

Your Honor, we are writing to ask the court not to kill our father, because that is exactly what a conviction would mean for him. We ask Your Honor to allow us to repay our father the debt we owe our parents. We ask you to guarantee his safety and the time we still have with him.

Respectfully yours,

They don't know how the trial would have gone if they hadn't written the letter. They know His Honor did read it.

Once they had all taken their seats in the courtroom, His Honor rose and in the presence of those gathered, gave the family his condolences and then proceeded to hold a trial that concluded with a suspended sentence.

The whole time, Father was clutching the handkerchief he'd used right after the crash to wipe the blood from his wife's forehead. He never learned what the letter said.

Have Mercy on Us

It was only the end of September, it wasn't clear yet if this was how things worked here, or if this was an unusual situation. Their faces were no more than fifteen centimeters apart and the gap between was thick with spittle shooting from the teacher's lips. He couldn't see it, but he could feel it landing on his face. He squeezed his mouth shut so it wouldn't get in. He was standing ramrod-straight and blinking. He would look at his aggressor for a while, then—as if in slow motion—close his eyes, wait two seconds, and open them again. It was the only way he could demonstrate his composure and simultaneously retain his dignity. The mounting fury gave him satisfaction and a desire to escalate. He just had to stand motionless and wait for his opponent to try and advance to the next stage. His honor was at stake; the cost was as yet unknown.

"Kyrie eleison," snarled his teacher. "Translate it into Polish!" he roared, having lost control over his nerves and tone of voice. "Who will have mercy on you?"

"Someone else, looks like," the student replied.

The teacher took half a step back. A trace of a grin appeared on the student's face, concealing derision.

"Do you think . . . Do you think the rules don't apply to you?" The teacher's face left no doubt he had flown completely off the handle.

"I'm not sure you really want to know what I think, Professor."

"You'll come in with your parents tomorrow morning."

"One of you has to come see my Polish teacher tomorrow."

They had grown accustomed to enjoying the time between parent-teacher conferences, so unexpectedly being called into school disturbed their precious peace.

"I'll go," his father said. "Can I just find out to what I owe this invitation?"

"I didn't know what 'kyrie eleison' meant."

"What does it mean?" asked Mom.

"You'd better not go then," said the son.

"Are you taking religion classes?" Father asked, unable to shake off his amazement.

"We're studying 'Bogurodzica,' those words come at the end of every verse."

"Kyrie eleison . . . No idea," pondered his father. "And this is what I'm supposed to talk to your Polish teacher about?"

"I didn't know what it meant, and the guy stood in front of me screaming bloody murder and kept spitting in my face."

"He spit in your face?" asked Mom, amazed.

"He didn't spit, but he was spitting. A fountain of saliva was shooting out of his mouth and every damn drop hit me in the face."

"We don't say 'damn,'" his father spoke up.

"How awful!" said Mom.

"In the morning we'll go into school together," said his father, concluding the conversation.

"Good morning, I hear you wanted to see me."

"I'd rather speak one on one."

"Yet I insist on speaking one on one on one," said Father.

"Yesterday your son was behaving unacceptably and if it happens again, I'll be forced to report him to the principal."

"I can see you're upset. Please tell me what happened."

"Your son deliberately refused to answer my question."

"And what was the question?"

"The class is currently studying the medieval poem 'Bogurodzica'. I asked him to translate the words 'kyrie eleison'; he stubbornly refused."

"Did you deliberately refuse to answer your teacher's question?" asked his father.

"I said I don't know what it means."

"How can anyone pretend not to know?" said the teacher, raising his voice.

"I don't know what it means either," replied Father calmly.

"Now I've heard everything!"

"And do you know what? I am also a teacher, I teach

university students. I follow the principle that I teach them first, and then I check to see if I succeeded."

"This is ridiculous! In every church you can hear those words several times a day."

"It just so happens that for his education we sent our son to school, not to church."

"You only need to go to church once a week to know what those words mean."

"And as a matter of fact we don't," said Father, looking the teacher dead in the eye.

"It seems like your attitude is going to cause your son a lot of trouble."

"My son has a lot of trouble, though not because of my attitude. But thank you for your feedback. Now I would just ask, Professor, if you would be so kind as to solve the riddle of 'kyrie eleison.' I'd prefer for my son to be prepared for his next class."

"Have mercy. Lord, have mercy."

"A perfect fit for our situation. Have mercy, Professor, on us unbelievers. Now I'll be going. We've sorted everything out, haven't we?"

"I'm telling you again that your son is going to get a lot of trouble in school."

"Didn't I already mention that my son does get a lot of trouble in school? Always has. Do you know he once twisted the arm of his geography teacher? Tell the professor."

"Dad, please, let's go."

"He twisted his teacher's arm?"

"He sure did! I think that was in September, too. During a long recess they went out to the field and were playing soccer. They got into an argument and started shouting. The afore-mentioned geography teacher was on duty there. She went up to the boys and, as misfortune would have it, gave my son's ear a painful tug. Do you know what happened? He grabbed her by that arm, twisted it, and held it bent up like that, behind her back. I saw her afterward, because I got called into school that time as well. Let me tell you, she was a big woman! Anyway, he was holding her by that arm, all the kids were cheering him on, because she was known for that sort of sadistic behavior, and he, poor kid, was standing behind her and didn't know what to do. As you can imagine, the situation didn't improve at all as the minutes went by. He was afraid to release her, because he knew if she caught him again, he'd be done for. She was screaming to let her go, and spinning in a circle, and he kept trotting along behind her with that arm. Finally he let her go and ran away. The next day I was called in to talk to the principal. As you can see, I'm a good and responsible father, I keep in touch with the educational institutions my sons attend."

"Why are you telling me this?"

"I'm almost finished. I came in like she asked and, just as with you today, my son and I reported to the principal's office. The geography teacher was already there and, believe it or not, she also asked for my son to leave the room, but I thought the conversation should include him. It was difficult and long. It took me a little time to explain that we weren't meeting about my son twisting a teacher's arm, but a teacher pulling my son by the ear."

"I feel these two situations are radically different," noted the teacher.

"And I happen to think they're not. Yesterday my son was also attacked by a teacher and it just so happens, professor, that that teacher was you."

For years to come, his parents regularly, if grudgingly, went to parent-teacher conferences, including with his Polish teacher. He never spoke a word to them. He often publicly named him as his worst student.

The last conference before graduation took place in the gymnasium with their whole class. Parents and teachers took their seats on evenly arranged chairs. Just after the principal's speech, the Polish teacher walked into the middle of the room. He was holding a thick folder of papers. He raised the microphone to his mouth and said:

"I'd like to invite up my worst student." He looked in the boy's direction and nodded. "Yes, you. Come on up."

The boy he'd called looked at his parents and stood up. In absolute silence he crossed the whole room and halted next to his Polish teacher.

"My worst student made me wait four years. Four long years without a shadow of hope. And suddenly at the very end of high school, he's written something worthwhile." He cast a look at the boy and patted him on the back. "See, on Isaac Babel you can do it."

Day of Atonement

He flew into Paris the day before the conference started; his colleagues had made plans to take him out.

"You have to" or perhaps rather "it would be impolite not to," that's what they said. He felt a little hurt, but he understood. They took him out to dinner and talked a lot about how much they respected him. They really appreciated what he'd contributed to science thus far, and that he had so many talented students. They raised the first toast to his latest publication, the second to the wonderful team he'd spent years building.

He sat surrounded by scientists he esteemed. He'd collaborated with many of them, and the rest he recognized from conferences and articles.

It was late spring in Paris, the low sun peeked over their table at the back of the elegant restaurant. He knew what they wanted to say, but he didn't make it any easier for them. He listened carefully, as always. He squinted slightly, set his jaw, felt his pulse slowly rise and his throat tighten. He felt touched by the respect they were showing him, but he knew there was more to the role he found himself playing at this table. He also felt angry and misunderstood. The blackmail to which he was shortly meant to capitulate was bringing a certain phase of his life to a close.

They were trying to be sensitive, so they spread out their actions over time. They had from the aperitif to the coffee to fit it all in. The choice of a French restaurant was deliberate. Aperitifs, hors d'oeuvres, the main course, salad, cheese, fruit, dessert, coffee. It was no coincidence they hadn't gone for a German *Eintopf.* They were physicists, so they were conscious of the paucity of Delta-T time, in which all the important words were meant to be spoken.

"You've formed a fantastic group of young scientists. You of all people know how badly we want them to join our labs. They'll bring the independent thinking that you've cultivated in them. They're attentive, because you've taught them to listen deeply to their collaborators' arguments. They know how to defuse the tension on a team, you've armed them with a whole arsenal of jokes that, when deployed at the right moment, bring the group back into balance. You and your team are at all the conferences that matter. Nearly all."

• • •

They were finishing the salad while the waiter was collecting the dirty plates, preparing the table for the cheeseboards to come out, and opening a new bottle of wine.

He said thank you and declined the next glass. He was tired of hearing how wonderful he was, he kept waiting for them to get to the point. He knew they'd have to fit it into the cheese course, to leave themselves a little time to smooth things over and leave a good impression, in spite of everything.

"We'd like to encourage you to come to the conferences that take place in Germany. You get invited, you never come. Not you and not your students. You're putting everyone in a very awkward situation. Them and us. We understand that your experiences in the war . . ."

"You don't understand now and you won't understand in the future. I'll go to Germany for the next conference."

Silence fell. The goal was achieved, the desserts had lost their sweetness.

Nearly forty years had passed since the end of the war.

He placed his open suitcase on the sofa. He had three days

until his departure. He packed methodically, not forgetting anything. As always, he used his Parker 51 to write out a list. He added item after item in navy-blue Pelikan ink.

Just before walking out the door, he glanced in the mirror, wishing to see a proud professor. He saw a well-dressed man, and in the background, his wife and two sons. He turned around, kissed everyone on the head and said:

"I'm going to visit the Germans, I hope I come back. See you in five days."

And he walked out of the house.

On the train he looked over the paper he was meant to give at the conference. He ate a sandwich and had some tea from his thermos. He crossed the border at night. The combination of darkness, loud announcements in German over the station PA system, the faces of border guards in tall official caps, and the barking of dogs put him on the edge of fleeing. He didn't sleep a wink until morning. He disembarked at the German station and rode to his hotel. There he unpacked his suitcase, hung his ironed shirts up in the wardrobe, showered and went to bed. He was awakened in the early afternoon by shouts from outside. He got up, pulled back the sheer curtains and opened a window. There was a protest taking place outside his hotel. On the placards he saw only one slogan: RELEASE HESS.

He went to the wardrobe, took his shirts off the hangers,

folded them up again and put them in his suitcase. Ten minutes later he saw in the hotel room mirror a terrified well-dressed man with a suitcase.

He turned around and went up to the wardrobe. He unpacked his clothes a second time and left the room.

The next day, he returned home, took out his hastily packed, wrinkled shirts and went to sleep.

From then on, his students started going to conferences in Germany.

Hanukkah

It was a strange invitation. His friend told him to come because she needed a specialist. He was neither an architect nor a builder; he didn't really understand what his role would be. He went out of curiosity.

"I know there should be a tunnel, but I don't know where the exit should be. You see those bushes, there, far off, beyond the line of trees? Maybe there?"

"From there you can only go uphill."

"Is that bad?"

"Fleeing uphill?"

"Yeah, I guess they'll catch us quickly."

"Unless you're fleeing at night, then it can be anywhere."

"That's the thing, we can't be sure when we'll have to escape. We've also got various hiding places prepared. Double walls, a windowless attic; in the cellar we made an invisible passage that goes beyond the footprint of the house. We've dug a ten-meter tunnel, with nice props to hold it up. That leads out to a bunker that's got everything we need to survive for a few days."

"History has seen such constructions before."

"Best to use good models."

"I don't know if it was the models that were bad, or if something else went wrong, but those bunkers' owners mostly didn't get to them in time."

"We will."

"That's good, I'd started to worry it was all for naught."

"No need to tease. Any advice?"

"What advice can I give you? So far I've never gone into hiding, never fled."

"So far."

"Sure, so far. And what about a second exit for this bunker of yours?"

"Maybe."

"Maybe it's got one, or maybe you should build one?"

"Maybe there should be one."

"There should always be a plan B."

"Our plan B is what I'm telling you now: hiding places, a bunker and a tunnel. We didn't think about a plan B for our plan B."

"Who's building all this for you?"

"A handyman and his team."

"One handyman and one team?"

"Well, yeah."

"Well then it's not worth a damn. Every hiding place should be made by a different handyman with a different team, and at the end I suppose you should kill them all so they don't spill the beans."

"Are you out of your mind? He's our neighbor!"

"And who do you want to hide from?"

"We don't know yet, exactly, but at the end of the day, from bad people. Do you think . . . ?"

"No, but I've come across a few stories about neighbors."

"Well, sure."

"Have you been on vacation recently?"

"I wish, we've been redoing this house for years. Anything we touch falls apart. We've rented a cottage up the road and we spend all day drawing plans. Entrance here, bedroom here, bathroom here, fireplace here, and then we shrink every room and see where we can build a hiding place. And a hiding place means ventilation, water, and septic system, because you don't know how long you'll be stuck there."

"Have you needed to hide before, but not had a place to?"

"People stood out in front of the house shouting 'get out!' but they didn't come inside. We were scared out of our wits and that was when we decided we needed this renovation. Let them see we're not going anywhere, we're going to keep living here."

"So it's because of them?"

"It started with them. It dawned on us that things won't necessarily be peaceful and safe forever. We're not so smug as to think that in our lifetimes in particular everything will just happen to work out. It was them that time, but next time other people might come, more government-type ones for instance."

"Are you scared?"

"No, we're doing it for our own satisfaction. Imagine: the moment arrives, we can sense they're about to come in, and we hide in our very best spaces and listen to them prowling all over the house. We've got supplies for a week, they can't find us anywhere, we smile at one another and think of Hanukkah, of the people who managed to wait it out. But you're right, it's not the best if after we leave to have to flee uphill. Though maybe better uphill than not at all?"

Enfilade

For as long as he could remember, she'd said it was hard work to live easy.

Her apartment was on the second floor of an old building, in a good neighborhood in Paris. You'd walk up a wooden spiral staircase that smelled like citrus-scented cleaning fluid.

You might stand at the door for hours; sometimes she'd open up, sometimes she wouldn't, you never knew. You might think she was malicious or—in the milder version—odd.

With age, she kept growing more helpless and less predict-able. Sometimes she'd pick up the phone and you'd manage to make lunch plans with her, but there were weeks when you might call constantly and get nothing. Sometimes you'd make plans and she wouldn't open the door anyway.

The older she got, the more often she didn't pick up the phone because she was in the hospital. She had a chronically bad leg. She wasn't supposed to walk, but she did. When asked how her leg was doing, she'd say she'd stopped caring long ago. Most often, she'd fall right near the pharmacy, and an ambulance would bring her to a hospital. When she was there you wouldn't hear a peep, you'd have to call around all the hospitals to find her. She treated visits under these circumstances as nothing special, as if she saw her family every day. The nurses would grumble that she was mean, she could be aggressive. After she whacked her roommate with her cane, she was moved to a single room. It had the look of a deliberate stratagem, and the outcome satisfied her greatly.

After yet another fall, she didn't go back to her apartment— she moved into a Jewish retirement home, outside central Paris. She had her own room, clothes and jewelry. She hated that place and the people who worked there. The retirees were mainly Ashkenazi Jews, while the staff was primarily made up of Black women with the patience of angels. The facility's official language ended up being Yiddish. The patients had long ago forgotten French, which was their second, third, or even fourth language; they exclusively used the tongue they knew from their family homes. The visitors didn't know Yiddish, making their only chance of communicating with their own grandparents the African Frenchwomen, who spoke it fluently.

She lived in the home for many years. She didn't want to talk to her family when they visited. Sometimes she spat on them.

She held bottomless reserves of sadness inside, which she had learned to convert into anger. For the last thirty years she'd been saying she didn't want to live anymore. She'd lived much longer than she would have liked. Now the only thing guarding the entrance to her apartment was a lock; you could go right in, no need to face anyone down.

The door opened inward and obstructed almost the entire hallway. The stench of fried fish perennially hung in the air. Immediately to the left was a dark, microscopic room with a toilet, and one meter further along, a separate bathroom, equally dark. The shower stall was on a forty-centimeter-high platform, and it was hard to imagine how she could climb in. On the right was a sliding door to a tiny kitchen with a window. The whole apartment was made up of three rooms in enfilade. First came the dining room, with a sideboard, a table, and a foldout desk with many drawers. The prevailing scent was the chemical odor of silver polish. This place became embedded in his memory while her second husband was still alive. The lunches the couple held for their Warsaw cousins, as they called the two brothers, forever became part of their culinary education. At this table they ate shrimp for the first time, here they learned how to slice cheeses and what order to eat them in. Artichokes, mussels, wines, and an amazing glass coffeemaker on an alcohol burner, which would appear at the end of every meal in the center of the table. Sometimes from the dining room you could hear her in the kitchen talking to her children. Everyone knew that they, along with her first husband, had been killed in the war.

When it transpired that the only chance of improving her second husband's health was a diet lacking salt or fat, all the delicacies on the home menu disappeared. Family gatherings now went differently. Lunch moved from noon to two. This was very un-French, but her husband wanted to follow his doctor's orders and had decided to do a lot of walking. At noon, he would collect his little Warsaw cousins and go out for a pre-lunch constitutional.

"We're going to get lunch," he informed them spiritedly when he took them on their first walk.

"Aren't we eating at home?" asked the two boys.

"I'm taking you to a restaurant. There we'll eat delicious things, and for the healthy stuff, we'll go back home."

They were torn between their loyalty to their aunt and curiosity about what was about to happen. Within ten minutes they were sitting in an Alsatian restaurant. Glistening before them was a platter of oysters. The next course was the heaviest pearl in the crown of Alsatian cuisine—choucroute, sauerkraut with a mountain of pork.

"Get to work, boys!" their uncle commanded with a grin. "We've got to hurry, because your aunt is waiting with lunch."

They ate, though never with such zest and pleasure as he did.

"Is this food good for your health?" the younger cousin asked.

"For my health, no, but it sure is wonderful for my palate!"

"Auntie said if you eat away from home, you'll die."

"And you think I'll live forever otherwise? All of us here are only passing through. And neither of you had better breathe a word once we're home! We're about to go have a healthy lunch and please don't fuss, just be good and eat everything at your aunt's. And next week we'll come here again."

They returned home and sat down in the dining room. Their aunt served boiled vegetables and steamed fish. Without salt. There was no cheese or dessert. Or coffee, either. And so it was until their uncle's death.

Past the dining room was the TV room. It smelled of the damp papers that lay on the bottom shelves of the library. A narrow sofa bed; two small, bulging armchairs with upholstered footrests; a rug; and a wonderful Telefunken-brand TV on a special one-legged table. To the right of the screen was a little door that locked with a tiny set of keys and concealed the buttons and the dial. It was in this room that the young cousins would spend the night when they came to visit their aunt and uncle.

When they could hear regular snoring in two voices from the bedroom, they'd turn on the TV. They'd turn the volume all the way down, so they could barely hear it, but they'd savor

the late-night adult movies. The sofa bed was neither too narrow, nor the sound too quiet.

The last room was the bedroom. It had a large, high bed set in
the corner, a nightstand, a wardrobe. Guests were forbidden
from entering it.

Now one could go in and inhale the intense stench of
mothballs. Once—long ago, when uncle was still alive—
sometimes it was allowed to follow him and help him take his
stamp albums from the lower shelves of the wardrobe.

"If you don't snitch to your aunt about our lunches, I'll
leave you the stamps in my will."

"And what will we do with them?" they'd ask, not knowing
how much the collection was worth.

"If someone's giving, you should take; at worst you'll throw
it out," he'd reply with a smile.

A few people came to their aunt's funeral, descendants of
people she knew from her hometown in Poland. Half of
what was written on her grave was false. All that was true
were the last name she got from her second husband and
her date of death. Her date of birth and maiden name
were the results of the turmoil of the first half of the
twentieth century.

• • •

One of the cousins who used to go out for lunch with uncle at noon invited the mourners to the Alsatian restaurant. They didn't feel like driving, so they chose a tiny bistro squeezed in between funeral parlors, just by the cemetery.

"Your aunt didn't talk much about herself," opened the most senior of the guests.

"She was my mother's aunt," replied the cousin.

"Tell us her story," pressed the elder.

The cousin thought for a little while, then replied, "Her story was her own creation."

"She didn't tell us anything."

"And that's how it'll stay. L'chaim!" The cousin lifted his glass of red wine in a toast.

After the funeral he went to the empty apartment for the last time. He passed the stinking entryway, the deserted dining room, and sat down on the narrow sofa bed in the TV room. He knew he'd never come back here. He glanced toward the bedroom and saw the wardrobe, where the promised stamps were meant to await him. He got up, dodged around the chairs' footrests and stopped in front of the closed cabinet. He turned the key and opened both doors, laying bare the whole interior. He leaned over to peer onto the lower shelves. On the top two lay the stamp albums. On the lowest, two little cases of brown polished leather. One held an eight-millimeter camera, the other, a projector. After taking both out, on the shelf there remained a cardboard box with the Kodak logo, under which someone had calligraphed in red marker "La Grande Bouffe." He drew the curtains, closed the bedroom door, and set the projector on the bed. He inserted the film, pointed the lens at the wall above the pillows, and pressed play. He saw a color film of himself at the Alsatian restaurant. He was sitting at a high table, wearing a brown sweater that read "Le Grand Prix." The whole space between him and the camera was taken up by a huge platter of oysters. He smiled joyfully at the camera, then took one oyster and tried to press it into his younger brother's mouth. There were three shots like this, and in one his brother didn't eat the proposed delicacy. In the next, his smiling younger brother was scarfing down tomatoes. When the choucroute arrived at the table, their uncle clearly handed the camera to the waiter, who filmed a one-minute panorama from the youngest gourmand to the oldest. The film ended with a wobbly shot showing Uncle, still holding the camera, trying to pour some wine into his glass.

The whole thing lasted no more than three minutes.

He watched it four times, packed up the projector and left the apartment.

One gift from his aunt was this maxim: "You have to give people happy stories, so they don't ask about sadness. False ones, ideally, so no one doubts they're true."

Vegetabling

The first time was a surprise. For him. She didn't realize. Good thing, too; it would have hurt her. He briefly considered saying something but decided against it. He was surprised this had come now, so early. Mom was sixty and had a memory like an elephant's. She remembered every story and could tell them without missing the tiniest detail. And now suddenly, bam!—she told him the same thing twice in one conversation. He was thirty-four, an age where deep reflection unfortunately came rarely, and definitely didn't involve his parents. His parents were something self-evident, constant and indestructible. But all of a sudden Mom had flipped into another category. No major event had occurred, but a door had cracked open whose existence he hadn't realized before, and as he peered through the narrow gap, he was suddenly changed. No longer a child, but someone internally prepared to worry about the future. He thought then that when a person forgets what they've just said, it's the start of a downward slope. Life went on, but his vigilance was enhanced. Every

77

now and again she happened to repeat herself; nothing serious, just the next stage.

Over the two years that passed between that event and her death, they had time to talk about many things to do with aging and passing away. The subject somehow raised itself. She said that there were people who wanted to live a long time, but she could only live under her own conditions.

"No vegetabling, remember, you can't let me lie there like an eggplant. Promise me you won't let that happen."

Of course he promised, fairly enthusiastically, even. After all, he didn't want her to be an eggplant.

She lost her life in a car crash in November; she died in December. Between those dates she was an eggplant, and he didn't know how to keep his word. In his defense, for a short time he believed she'd return to health and consciousness. Besides, he didn't know how to kill a mother in the ICU.

No one is prepared for the death of a loved one; he was so very unprepared that the funeral was held in the presence of over a hundred people in total silence. Not speaking makes sense—it is emptiness—but this wordlessness wasn't deliberate. He simply hadn't found the inner strength for writing or speaking. In that hush, in the cold and falling snow, he crossed into the next stage of his life, resigned that now it was his father who'd start repeating his stories again and again.

It no longer surprised him; he now knew that danger could come from where you least expected it.

When someone in a family dies, it forces a reshuffle, or rather you have to be prepared for changes. The loss must be filled with something. First with mourning, later with attempting to return to life.

He'd just discovered that time is merciless, and you never know who has how much left. He saw that promising his parents euthanasia wouldn't relieve anyone's anxiety. It had worked once, it wouldn't again.

Here began the period of chronophobia and conversations with Dad. He wanted them both to feel fulfilled while they still had time. For each to learn as much about the other as possible. Who were you with before Mom? Who was Mom with before you? What were your crises as a couple like? How did you manage to live, after what you went through in the war? Did you understand your parents? Why did you and Janek fall out so suddenly? Do you regret us living in Poland?

He encouraged his father to ask questions too, and sometimes it worked. Well, do you regret that we didn't leave Poland? Explain to me why you didn't want to study. I didn't always understand you; more often, Mom did. I think you're like her, do you agree? I see you're raising your children differently than we raised you boys, aren't you afraid to give them so much freedom? Can you see now that you never stop being scared for your own children? I'm really worried that you'll have nothing to live on in a few years. Do you ever think about that? Wouldn't you like to write with a fountain pen? Why don't I buy you one for your birthday? And maybe you'd like a blazer too, at least one?

He learned to enjoy moments weighted with the risk of loss. He spent time with his dad and grew ever more scared. He knew that this fear was poisonous, but he had no doubt it would stay with him forever.

Dad died fifteen years after mom. He vanished just like her, suddenly. It wasn't a crash; for him, fate chose the ocean.

At the funeral he read a eulogy. It began with the words: "The first time was a surprise."

Sukkot

For a while he had a last name ending in "-ski"; such were the times. Ski's son also had an interim Ski name, and a temporarily Ska wife. Later everything went back to normal—as some people like to call the times that come after cataclysms.

Old Ski—before he got old—knew that interwars don't last forever and have the somewhat frequent tendency to end abruptly, out of the blue. This knowledge can lead to two types of behavior. The first is to live in fear, the second—to live for the moment. He used to fear for the lives of his parents, brothers and sisters, as well as his closer and more distant cousins. His anxiousness did them no good. So he bet on a life between the tragedies that he knew would regularly arrive.

He lived hygienically. He washed his hands very frequently. Maybe even more than twenty times a day. This is how doctors have behaved since Semmelweis. In his medical bag, apart from a stethoscope, a thermometer, a prescription pad and a stamp reading "Prof. Ski, Physician," he carried Cellucotton and a tiny bottle of spirit for disinfecting his hands.

Every morning he went to the hospital where he'd been working since the start of the current interwar. Punctually at two o'clock he closed the door to his office and, after descending three flights of stairs, walked out in front of the hospital, where every day the same taxi driver would be waiting for him. They'd known each other for years; they didn't talk much. Within ten minutes they'd arrive at Ski's house. The doctor would get out, nod to the taxi driver, and enter the stairwell. He'd go up two floors on foot. In his apartment he'd greet his wife, open the door to his study, place his doctor's bag on the armchair, and close the door. He'd undress, put on his pajamas, get into bed, and immediately fall asleep. After fifteen minutes he'd get up, dress, take his bag, say goodbye to his wife, and go downstairs to the taxi, which would be waiting right by the entrance. The driver would fold up his newspaper, start the engine, and return to the hospital without a word. So it was for years, until one day the department head called him in.

"My dear colleague, for many years I've watched you go

home at two o'clock, day after day. What would you think, dear colleague, if we placed a foldout sofa in your office for you, where you could enjoy your daily nap without any need to leave the hospital?"

"Am I some fucking deadbeat who sleeps on the job?" replied the doctor.

The department head conceded that Professor Ski was not a fucking deadbeat, and never repeated his proposal.

He observed hygiene in every area of life. He only slept with women he was absolutely certain were healthy. He didn't risk his health or his life unnecessarily. He cherished both too much.

He sometimes had housekeepers who—until they met a handsome soldier from the unit next door—gave him a great deal of pleasure, and who got no shortage of excitement themselves. Two doors separated the servant's room behind the kitchen from the rest of the apartment. The household pretended these were soundproof.

Ski frolicked through the life he'd regained. He knew that not everybody's days were numbered alike. He didn't believe in the Almighty, and He repaid Ski with indifference. The doctor's prior experience suggested to him that faith didn't make God exist. If at some point he discovered otherwise, he intended to be ready with apologies.

He worked in his profession for sixty-five years, enjoying respect in his field and also among his patients. He had a reputation as a Don Juan. Despite being over ninety years old, many women flashed him flirtatious smiles. To the end of his days he took perverse satisfaction in the hateful glances of betrayed husbands.

Two years before he died, he drove his latest wife to such a loose end that she kept phoning his daughter-in-law to ask for support. Despite his advanced age, Professor Ski's libido was undiminished. His much younger new spouse was terrified that during the act of love, he might suddenly expire. The daughter-in-law was not fond of the doctor. She left Ska-number-whatever's pleas for help unanswered.

By the end of his life he'd repeatedly called an ambulance to his house. When the breathless doctors raced in wearing not-quite-spotless aprons, he'd grill them on their hygiene. He'd force them to wash their hands and apologize for their lack of professional standards. After yet another intervention, the ambulance refused to keep coming to the doctor's address.

• • •

His last wife phoned his son asking him to come right away. He called his own son, and in an hour they were sitting by the bed that held a very old and wrinkled Ski. Even though in recent years he'd shrunk a few centimeters, he now looked skinnier. He seemed practically embalmed. He hadn't spoken a word in several days. He didn't want to eat; he was only taking fluids. His eyes were shut and his breath, quick and shallow. His son and grandson sat there in silence. It was clear that now only one thing could occur. They called the ambulance service, which was nursing a grudge and refused to come.

"This past year he started talking a lot about holidays," said his last wife, out of the blue. "He'd talk about how his mother escaped and hid all through Sukkot, then the last day she went to the Gestapo, because she couldn't live like that any longer."

The curtains, illuminated beautifully by the setting October sun, bore the shadows of a few tall cactuses.

Suddenly, the body that had looked incapable of any effort sat up and spoke eight final words:

"Ski is the smartest person in the world."

Grandpa's Sisters

They knew father was about to arrive; they'd barely finished in time. The younger one stayed in the bathroom, and the elder, driven by desperate bravado, went to open the door.

They stood facing one another; the father was nearly forty-five, the elder son, eighteen. Father's once lush black head of hair—he always said he was the bane of barbers—was now but a memory. Thick, coarse hair circled his head, forming a noble wreath. On top, it was long gone. His son, only in pants, stood before him proudly. With his brother's help, he'd just successfully created a precise copy of their father's hairdo. The younger boy had warned him it would end badly; the older one was counting on their father's sense of humor. He'd misjudged. His father glanced at him, took off his shoes, moved him out of the way with his hand so he could leave the hallway, and went into his room. He didn't say a word.

"I told you he'd think we were making fun of him."

"I thought he had more of a sense of humor. I didn't do it to be mean, I wanted us to laugh together."

"It clearly didn't work."

"Will you help me shave off the rest?"

"No, I've had enough excitement for one day."

He didn't know that shaving a head with lots of long hair growing on it should be done in stages. First you have to shorten it as much as possible, and only then shave it.

He came out of the bathroom two hours later. He was bald, but he didn't seem happy about it. He looked scalped, and to make matters worse he had no one to blame but himself. After a few hours the wounds dried, and a huge scab started to cover his head. Within two days, there was no doubt a doctor was unavoidable.

"Go to the hospital with him," Mom said to Dad.

"If he's so independent, he can go himself."

"Take him!"

They got in the car without a word; his father was still sulking. They sat down on wooden chairs in the hallways of the dermatology department and waited in silence. In front of an office, a group of fifteen young people in lab coats was gathering. A half an hour later, the door opened. In the doorway stood an older lady with a large magnifying glass dangling over her breasts like a precious medallion. They went into her large office.

"You used to be so handsome," said the doctor, starting with Father. "You've fattened up like a pig."

Dad wasn't happy, but he valiantly bore her impertinence. The stroking of his cheeks was harder to take. He tried to pull away, unsuccessfully. She inspected his face close-up, as if seeking something within it.

"You've gone all pudgy-wudgy. But you still look like your father. Pull yourself together, you need to lose weight. But all right, tell me what brings you here."

Without asking permission, he whipped off his son's cap. The doctor took one look and grinned.

"Today's my lucky day! Hold on, I'll call my students.

"Sit on this little stool. Ladies and gentlemen, please examine this patient. You have five minutes, then each of you will write down your diagnosis. We'll treat this as a test."

He sat with his head down, while terrified students, male and female, circled him. He felt silly and awkward; he was barely two or three years younger than they were. Once his father and the doctor stepped a little to the side, he was inundated with pleas to reveal his diagnosis. He didn't know what was wrong, so to them he stopped existing. They kept coming up with their magnifying glasses and peering at him.

"End of examination, you won't get any more ideas. Please leave your signed sheets of paper on my desk."

• • •

The doctor waited until everyone had left, then went up to her desk and looked through the responses.

"Of the whole bunch, one girl's a dermatologist, the rest are morons."

She prescribed an antibiotic and stroked Dad's head.

"If you lost weight, you'd look like him physically, but I can see you haven't got that glint in your eye."

"You're going to the follow-up on your own," said Dad in the car.

He went to the follow-up appointment with Mom; the doctor didn't even look at her.

"See there, I helped you! Show me up close, show me your eyes. How old are you? Yep, fit as a fiddle. Take your mom and go on back home."

When a few years later Dad was in the hospital after a stroke, the son called a doctor they knew; she was a neurologist and, off-duty, the dermatologist's sister.

"No use telling me over the phone. Come pick me up and we'll go see your father."

Fifteen minutes later he was in front of her house, twenty minutes after that they were walking into the hospital.

"Take me to the department head," she said in a voice that would brook no opposition.

They walked down a long hallway past a row of open doors. In every room there lay motionless patients. At the end they turned left and stopped in front of a door reading "Head of Department."

"What are you waiting for? Open it."

He knocked.

"Don't knock, open it!"

She strode past the surprised secretary, and he followed her.

"Sit down, missy," she barked in the secretary's direction, "and mind your own business."

She opened the next door.

"Oh, Professor," said the surprised department head at her desk. "What brings you here?"

"They made you department head? Can't believe my eyes."

The department head stood up and the professor immediately sat down in her place.

"Bring me the medical documentation for patient—" and here she gave his father's name.

When the two of them were left alone, she looked around the office. She opened a desk drawer and immediately closed it again with disgust.

"You know how to get your way, I see. Just like your

grandfather. Don't worry, we'll take care of your father. We'll do everything ourselves; we can't rely on her. I don't know how she ended up here, she flunked three of my exams."

Three months later his father left the hospital.

A few weeks after that she phoned.

"What, you don't call anymore?" she said cheerfully. "When you needed me, you'd call whenever you liked. Relax, I'm joking. Bring me your father's case report, I have something floating around in my mind."

He went to his father's, got the hospital documentation and brought them to the professor.

"I like you," she said. "You know I'm not easy, people are scared of me, but you picked up the phone and didn't even leave me a second to think. You told me to get myself together and drove me to the hospital."

"I asked politely. I was really terrified."

"Politely? Too bad I didn't record it, you'd hear how polite it was! But I'll tell you, I appreciated that you were so decisive. You didn't send your mother, you sorted it out yourself. I could sense I wouldn't be able to say no, and you must know I don't often feel that way."

"Thank you very much."

"You're very welcome. Now, you realize I knew your grandfather well?"

"Yes. And apparently your sister knew him pretty well too."

"Apparently, exactly. You're cheeky, like your red-headed grandfather."

"Grandpa was happy that I wasn't born a redhead."

"It isn't only transmitted through hair color."

"What?"

"A redheaded personality. Did you bring your father's documentation?"

He'd gathered up a little of it. He lay a few folders on the small table by her armchair.

She read for a long time, looking everything over again and again.

"Do you remember if your grandfather had a lady friend in oncology?"

Dad's Dog

Everyone has the right to make decisions about their own lives, but there's no rule that others will find them easy to take.

As soon as he heard, he called his father. It was the first time they'd spoken in a year.

"Is it true?" he asked.

"It is," replied his father.

"I'll be right over."

A half hour later the three of them were sitting face to face. The second son sighed with relief, because he'd gotten sick of showing evenhanded understanding.

Grandpa's supply of medical lady friends had run out, so they needed to search on their own.

A nearly inoperable tumor, a very difficult procedure for someone with his history. They found a surgeon who took on the hazardous task despite the complexities.

Father died during the procedure. Resuscitation returned

him to life. Then he arrested—as doctors say—a second time, in the recovery room. It worked again.

When his sons visited him, he was intubated, but conscious. To communicate, he used a marker and a little whiteboard. He wrote that there was a dog in the room. They gave one another a surprised look, then glanced around the room. Nothing, no trace of a dog. Their father got annoyed and kept scrawling.

There was a dog being treated in this room, now they've taken him away momentarily for tests. No, he wasn't in a bed. He had a special dog pen. He was in really bad shape because he'd had a tough operation.

The sons nodded.

The next day their father was doing a little better. He was breathing on his own, the respirator tube had been removed. He was having a hard time speaking, his throat and esophagus were sore, but he went back to the story about the dog.

"He's still here, but I'm telling you, he's barely alive. He's really brave. Yesterday they brought him back from testing so exhausted that he slept eighteen hours straight."

While talking to the department head, one of the sons asked about the dog.

"What dog?"

"The one in the room with our dad."

"Have you two seen a dog in there?"

"No, but Dad's mentioned it many times. We feel a little awkward saying this, but we'd rather the dog was treated at a different facility."

"Your dad told you, huh? All right, we'll take the dog away, no problem."

"Thank you very much, doctor. We appreciate it. I have a good friend who also works in the ICU and I know what a tough job it is."

"Oh, that's very kind. What's your friend's name?"

The sons told him the friend's name and which hospital he worked at, then left content.

Each of them returned to his own home and in both a similar scene unfolded. They told their wives about the dog, and the wives jeered at them for their boundless faith in their father's words.

Some while later, one son got a call from his friend, the ICU doctor.

"How's your dad?"

"Thanks for asking. It looks like he's on the mend. You won't believe it, there's a dog in Dad's room."

"Shit, I was hoping it wasn't true! My friend who's in charge of your father called and was rolling on the floor, laughing his butt off telling me that nonsense. I'm begging you, stop talking about the dog. There's no dog in there; your dad is pumped up on all kinds of amazing meds. And if you're going around spouting crap like that, then for fuck's sake, leave me out of it!"

"Don't you boys think I've forgotten about that dog," said Dad at one Sunday lunch, many months later.

Meta-Sized

"Within five days I knew," he heard from the other side of the hotel wall.

A summer evening, late, but bright, the window open; you could hear everything.

Some close the windows so they don't hear, others, just the opposite—they'd happily go from room to room, opening everyone's windows wide, so they won't miss a single word.

He was glad that things behind the wall were getting promising. He didn't need to listen to an hours-long quarrel, just a few moments would do. He was of an age where stories from his own past rarely came to mind on their own. He needed a catalyst, a sentence, a smell; often the right light was enough.

He was lying in a bed he hadn't made himself, and which tomorrow he'd leave to someone else to make for him. He didn't expect to get a good night's sleep in it.

"You knew what?"

"That marrying you was a bad idea," came the reply.

• • •

That was all he needed from them now; the voices drifted into the background.

"With you I can be who I wish I was," he'd said many years ago in a quiet room.

It was almost dark, so objects had lost their colors but still had their shape. His words hung in the safe gloom; they needed no answer. When he heard himself, shame bore away his momentary happiness. It had sounded much more selfish than he had been prepared to accept. He'd mistaken nostalgia for dreams of the future, and now everything together was fit for only that room and nothing more—no place, no time. He left before the colors returned. They were gone very briefly; it was also summer then.

He fell asleep early in the morning. When he woke up, he could only hear the bustling of the city. He went into the bathroom and wondered for a while whether the shower floor was clean enough to stand on without sandals, which he'd forgotten to pack. A quick shower, a fresh shirt, and the elevator down to a hotel coffee. A glance at the sausages and bacon was plenty for breakfast. He went out for a walk; there were a few hours to go until the afternoon event.

"Most of all I'd like to learn how to send photos."

"This is what you do, ma'am. You've got to go into your pictures, choose one, and then this little icon will appear at the bottom . . ."

"I'll pick this one from Elżunia's funeral; or, no, I'll take this one from yesterday, from Krysia's funeral. Boy, did she suffer."

"All right, so let's take Krysia . . ."

"Not Krysia, her funeral. She was always healthy, I mean more than any of us, and suddenly . . . she got sick! But not like a cold or anything, she had cancer that got meta-sized."

"It got what?"

"Meta-sized, the kind that pops up all over a person."

The local community center; a twenty-year-old woman in jeans, Doc Martens and a red hoodie, and a woman in her seventies, wearing low wedge heels, a navy-blue skirt and a blazer. They're sitting in armchairs whose glory days were in the early seventies; once beautiful, now uncomfortable. Between them a triangular table—also of that era—stands on three thick hairpin legs. They're sitting as close to one another as the uncomfortable furniture will allow. They don't look like a grandmother and her granddaughter, more like a retiree who wants to catch up on what her phone can do, and a university student offering free support. On the wall behind them is a poster for this afternoon's author event.

●　●　●

He sits at a neighboring table and listens. He always arrives early, to avoid being late, to look and listen.

"You know what I'd like to learn? Apparently this is something you can do with your phone nowadays. Know what I've got in mind?"

"I don't, but I can't wait."

"Me neither. I dream of *learn-ing* . . . guess what? How to make obituaries on my phone and then send them around to everybody."

All of a sudden, a memory came back from years ago. He was abroad, he'd gone on a short work trip. After three days he got a text from Mom. "Still alive son." She'd had a phone for a while, but she hadn't yet learned how to type a question mark. He was very moved by this text, the quintessence of concern and the disarming need to be in touch. He was too young to know how to hold on to that feeling for longer; he wrote back quickly and teasingly: "Glad to hear it, Mom." The memory makes him feel embarrassed. He doesn't know how she reacted, he hopes she smiled, but actually he's afraid he hurt her. Once your parents are gone, such memories awaken a sense of guilt and helplessness. They remind you of conversations that would have gone differently today. They dump out a whole truckload of regret and remorse.

• • •

He went into the author event with the two women. He saw them, sitting right in front of him, in the first row, working for an hour and a half on an obituary.

After the event he went back to the hotel. He could have disappeared straight into his room, but he looked around the lobby and ambled over to an area where a few armchairs stood. He sat down in one of them, with some women and men behind him. He didn't know who they were to one another, which is why he'd chosen to sit near them in particular.

"I'm begging you, don't say you don't like his book again. It polarizes your readers, understand?"

He wasn't sure, but this sounded like the voice of the woman he'd heard the night before through the window. The one who knew within five days that marrying him was a bad idea.

"And don't be self-deprecating, because someone else will pile on and what will we do then?"

It was her, no doubt.

"Do?"

"Don't joke around, I'm telling you, it puts the audience off. Cheerfulness makes them jealous, and jealous people don't buy books."

"Let's go up to our room," said the writer. He cast an embarrassed glance across the lobby, got up and walked toward the elevators.

Too bad, he thought, I could have learned something. He got up and went back to his room.

He hadn't smoked in twenty years. He stepped onto the balcony and took out a cigarette. He'd been carrying around a sealed pack for two years. Health, sure, but freedom of choice above all. He sat down in a chair he'd brought out of the cramped room. Its uncomfortable upholstered back was shaped like a big chocolate bar, its seat—formerly also upholstered, now vintage, a fixer-upper—was hard, bristling with a forest of tiny nails. It matched neither the hotel's decor nor the quality of the remaining furniture. It had probably ended up here by accident. Maybe a repairman had brought it out of the storeroom instead of a ladder and had forgotten to return it.

He took a drag; smoking didn't give him as much joy as the very fact that he could do it.

"Well, I'd like to have the kind of stroke where afterwards I'd think everything was fine," said a familiar voice.

"Have you ever heard of a stroke like that?" asked the writer quietly.

"I'd like one where afterwards I could still rely on myself."

• • •

Yet another memory returned.

"Dad, what year were you born?"

"Fifteen thousand . . . ? "

"Not fifteen thousand. You were born in 1940. What year were you born?"

"Three?"

His father, a professor of science, had stopped understanding numbers. After his stroke he lost the ability to grasp even the concept.

"Dad, how old are you now?"

". . . one three?"

"Dad, you're fifty-eight years old. Repeat after me: fifty-eight."

"Ten two?"

Haunting memories from his school days returned. The two of them are sitting at the son's desk. The boy reads a problem:

"A projectile is fired from point A at an angle of thirty-five degrees. Velocity . . ."

"You understand you can describe the projectile's motion in two spatial axes, vertical and horizontal?"

"Yes."

"You also understand that in the horizontal axis the projectile moves at a constant velocity, right?"

"Yes."

"And the vertical?"

". . ."

"Come on, it's a body in free fall and has downward acceleration due to gravity, remember?"

"Yes."

His father solves it, all the while explaining what he's doing and why. Step by step.

"Do you understand what I'm doing now?"

"Yes."

"This is a diagram that describes parabolic projection, do you understand?"

"Yes."

"You insert the known quantities, simplify, solve, and there you have it. Next problem, read it out loud."

The son reads, the father writes down the data.

"You see why I've written it down this way?"

"Yes."

"Now you pick it up from here, when you're done, bring it to me, we'll take another look together."

The son tries to hold down the page with the problems his father was just solving. The father looks straight in his son's eyes and slowly slides the paper out from under his fingers. Despite the strong pressure, it disappears unharmed through the door, along with his father.

• • •

Not quite fifteen years later, he's sitting facing his sick father, and his emotions are cycling between revenge and mercy. He'd prefer to trade both for empathy, but it is what it is.

"Dad, you were born in 1940, at the very beginning of the war, which broke out in 1939."

His father raises his tear-filled eyes to him.

"Do you understand, Dad?"

"No."

"You were born in 1940. Do you understand?"

"No."

His gaze is helpless and sincere. It does not contain the cunning of a fraud trying to bluff past his own ignorance. He looks nothing like his son in his school days.

"Or a heart attack, but a painless one," says the voice of his hotel neighbor. "In general I'd like something that doesn't give me any trouble. Are there any diseases like that?"

Happiness

Happiness has many faces; he ended up with the most wonderful one.

The end of a sweltering June can be horrible, and this one was off the charts. The late-falling dusk brought only darkness, not relief. They were sitting around a fire pit; it never even crossed anyone's mind to light it. On the ground, leaning on one another as only people at that age do, using one another's bodies as makeshift bedding. Surrounding them were many half-empty bottles and a gentle cloud of marijuana smoke. Although he was twice their age, he sat among them, holding a glass of summer wine, not kidding himself for an instant that he was back in his twenties. He knew that some of them would leave in pairs, and some alone. For him there was no confusion, he understood exactly what group he belonged to. Maybe one more round of a joint passed from hand to hand, maybe another glass of increasingly warm wine, and the time would come to tactfully slip off.

"Dad, your phone." His daughter's sharp ears caught the sound of it vibrating.

One drag after another of relaxing smoke had dulled his curiosity.

"You not going to answer?"

He reached into his pocket. It wasn't ringing anymore. Three missed calls, all from the same unfamiliar number. He put the phone aside and returned to his exercises in happiness.

On his father's side of the family, they'd had nothing but boys; the very first girl in ninety years was this young woman sitting right next to him. He yet again suppressed the desire to hug her. He didn't risk making any gesture, he just reflected on his gratitude to her for being here together. His daughter glanced at him and embraced him tenderly. Something had changed in recent years, gestures like this now made emotion swell inside him and his eyes moist. The phone buzzed again. It was the same number calling. He was about to ignore it once more, when an avalanche of speculation cascaded through his mind: something's happened to somebody, maybe his wife, maybe his other child or his father. Probably his father. He didn't like this condition, which he could work himself into in the blink of an eye. Just a second ago he'd been blissful, now he couldn't keep his thoughts from barreling toward tragedy. Once again he peered at the unfamiliar number and answered.

"I'm sorry to bother you, but it's urgent. I don't know if you remember me, we went to university together."

He remembered.

"I'd like to tell you something. Recently I was doing some reading around the war and all that history. I remembered some stories my grandma's sister told me and somehow I can't stop thinking about you."

"Listen, it's nice to hear from you, but could this wait until tomorrow?" he said, leaning on a nearby shoulder.

"Did something happen?" whispered his daughter.

He shook his head, stood up, and took a few steps so he wouldn't bother her.

"I thought you'd be happy, I've got so much to tell you. They lived by the train tracks . . ."

Lucky me, he thought, getting to hear about train tracks at this very moment. The bliss that had held him tight just a few seconds ago had vanished without a trace. He had enjoyed those moments of pride blended with hope that there was more to life than feeling the weight of all his ancestors and their stories on his shoulders. For a moment he'd glimpsed an entirely new perspective: Maybe he could feel strength, and draw it from all of them? Maybe they were the ones carrying him?

". . . by the train tracks that led to a camp. The train

would slow down in their village, because there's a very sharp curve there."

All right, now tell me what happened there. The whole village ran out to help them? Brought them food and drink? Or instead took their valuables and didn't even offer a glass of water in return? Why do I have to hear these stories? He didn't even think to ask if I wanted this.

"People would gather along the tracks; they knew when the transports would come. Very often, just before that curve, individual Jews would jump out. Everyone prayed that they'd get away from the tracks in one piece. German soldiers sitting in special booths attached to the train cars would hunt them. If they hit an escapee, you'd have to wait until they allowed you to deal with the person. If anyone managed to dodge the bullets, then the time came for the Polish hunt."

"Thank you very much, that's enough."

"You don't want to hear the end?"

"We both know how it ended."

As he spoke to his university friend, he walked more than a hundred meters away from his daughter and her friends. Happiness remained behind at the unlit campfire. He was trying to remember how he'd felt before he picked up the phone. He remembered what it was, but the emotion had disappeared. He put his phone in his pocket.

"Hello! Hello!"

He thought they'd ended the conversation, but his friend was still talking.

"Oh, good, you're there. Something cut us off."

"Nothing cut us off, I thought you were done. Can we finish this conversation tomorrow?"

"Sure, I didn't want . . . I didn't think . . . I'm sorry, I'll call back."

He repocketed the phone, went back, and sat down. His daughter leaned on his back. After a few moments he was holding the joint. He took a drag and waited for that pre-conversation emotion to return. He held the smoke in his lungs a long time. She turned her head around and smiled.

"Things okay?"

He nodded. The first commandment in his paternal deca-logue was: thou shalt never worry thy children.

Why the hell did I say we'd finish the conversation tomorrow? he thought. Instead of hearing him out and thanking him for the story, I flew like a moth to a flame. An apt phrase.

"Can you talk now?" asked his college friend.

"I can."

"Is everything okay with you?"

"Is everything okay with anyone you've ever met?"

"I guess not, but it's just a saying. Don't you say that?"

"No, I'm doing my best to give up phrases that don't move the conversation forward."

"People often ask if everything's all right, so what do you answer when they do?"

"That things are bearable."

"Don't they expect you to satisfy their curiosity?"

"You can see yourself there's no expectation or curiosity in it."

"You've changed, you used to be more fun."

"I've gotten honest. Let's hear that story you started yesterday."

"First of all I'd really like to apologize again for pressuring you like that."

"Thanks."

"I'll tell you why I'm really calling."

There are two possibilities, he thought, your family either killed Jews or saved them. Too late for me to be fussy, you'll tell me anyway.

"Talk."

"Great, because yesterday you didn't sound so enthusiastic. Actually, you were talking so slowly it sounded like you were stoned."

"Astute diagnosis."

"Fair enough, but at our age . . ."

"At our age I recommend it even more. Tell your story."

"I was calling because I think we could do something together. I'll take you to that great-aunt of mine and you can chat. She doesn't like going back to it, but I'll tell her that maybe one of the trains that went by her house had your relatives on it."

"You know what? If she doesn't want to talk about it, maybe let's not pressure her. We'll both get by without it, somehow."

"Stop! We'll go, we'll bring a bottle of vodka, she'll put out some smalec and pickles, we'll talk."

"I don't really like smalec."

"It's okay, one time never hurt anybody. We've got to go and find out where exactly they buried the bodies. Then you come back with a rabbi or whoever, dig them out of the railroad embankment, and take them to your cemetery."

"The embankment?"

"Exactly, do you get it now?"

He certainly did. Yet he'd wanted to spend at least one moment in a happy world. I'm proud my daughter isn't embarrassed of me, I'm proud she wants to spend time with me, I'm proud . . . , he thought, and he dreamed that maybe sometime it would happen again.

Coffee Marks

"Yes? Hello? Have you got something to say to us?" he asked aggressively. "To what do we owe this interest?"

"Leave him alone," she said.

"Please don't be shy, let us in on the secret," he said, not giving up.

They'd always run into somebody who couldn't take their eyes off them. It was usually a person sitting at a neighboring table, watching them shamelessly, like a spectator in a theater. Someone who thought her trembling hands were a public pass to unceremoniously stare.

"Wait here a second, I'll get up and ask him what's going on." He pushed out his chair and at that moment the observer averted his gaze.

He never managed to get any further. Which was too bad; the pent-up energy could gnaw at him for a long time. He didn't lose hope, he was waiting for some risk-taker who'd let him put the finishing touches on his gentlemanly defense of dignity.

• • •

They drank their first coffee together in Venice. The cappuccinos lightly dusted with chocolate shavings were fantastic. They couldn't resist, they ordered another round, then some espressos as well. Before long they were just waiting for their pulses to even out. They hoped their hearts would give up trying to evacuate through their throats. In anticipation of steady breathing, they placed their empty cups upside down on paper napkins bearing the coffee producer's logo. As they left the café, they took these little sepia images with them—mementoes of their joint caffeine overdose. She was thirty-nine, he, thirteen; they were on a trip they both found disappointing, but which left good memories. She'd wanted to show him Italy, see the historic sites and visit the galleries together; she was expecting him to be a good companion. He wasn't. He got bored and let her down at every turn. She felt like she'd overestimated him; he was still a child, he couldn't feel at home in the world of architecture and painting. They disembarked in Padua. The train had been stopped there for so long that they gave up on riding further. Giotto's frescoes stayed in his memory because they were the first things he saw. He remembered them but found nothing interesting about them. What he found more impressive was the man they met on the street who flipped his dentures ninety degrees and opened his mouth. What he remembered of Florence was the giant line to the Uffizi Gallery and a switchblade knife she didn't want to buy him. In Venice they didn't pay for their accommodation in a small hostel. They packed up and walked out.

"You didn't pay?" he asked in disbelief.

"You want to keep going or are we turning back?"

They crossed the square, walked around the palace and sat down in the little café where the day before they'd been abusing caffeine. Their Italian expedition was coming to its end. She enjoyed her last good coffee, and he, the fact that they were finally going home. With a trembling hand she passed him her coin purse and asked him to take out some change.

Two years later he showed her a scene he'd filmed with his friends. A wooden vacation cabin, far too little light. He sits at a table, around his neck is a scarf. He holds one end in his left hand, the other in his right, which also clutches a glass of transparent liquid. His right hand is shaking hard, so hard he can't hold the glass without spilling it. His left hand slowly pulls the scarf downward, allowing the right hand with the glass to move gently to his mouth. The shot ends with success—he smiles as he drinks the contents of the glass.

"Your hands are shaking horribly."

"That was for the movie, it was a joke."

"It looks so realistic that no one will believe you."

He put the film in a drawer, and when years later he wanted

to show it to some people he knew, it was neither there nor anywhere else; it had disappeared without a trace.

Her hands had been shaking for as long as he could remember. When he was younger, he didn't notice; when he was growing up, he was embarrassed by how people looked at her. As an adult, he'd attack everyone who looked down their noses at the balancing acts she attempted in order to take even a little sip of coffee.

After a certain point he started bringing her a straw, so she could drink her espresso without splashing the whole table and herself. Over years they put together a remarkable collection. Every cup from which she'd splashed coffee, they'd place on a paper napkin, creating a stamp. They made these coffee marks on newspapers, handwritten papers, sometimes the pages of books. They all lay in a drawer, alongside her husband's pipes.

Her trembling hands spilled coffee as she talked about her husband. He'd had a stroke and returned home altered. Not for the worse, not for the better—he'd changed into someone else.

"Do you know how strange that is? Forty years of our

relationship went obsolete in a single day. I'm glad he survived and came back. Unfortunately that's not my husband. It's strange all of a sudden to have a new partner move in who, to make things even harder, looks exactly like your husband. Evening comes, we get into our bed, but it's not our bed. I mean, for him it is, but not for me, not anymore. I shouldn't be telling you all this, I'm sorry. Don't worry, it could be worse, after all. He survived, let's be glad."

"Are you going to split up?"

"Wash the cups so I don't smash them; you need to get going."

Their last coffee they drank in town, in a little Italian café.

"Did you draw that yourself?"

"Yes."

It was a design for some stairs that were meant to be installed in his new apartment.

"It looks good, shame you didn't go to art school."

"Shame you didn't tell me that earlier."

"I wanted you to get a high school diploma, speak French, and know how to swim, the rest I left up to you."

"Do you really regret I didn't go to art school? Do you wish we'd had the same profession?"

"I'm more worried about whether you're happy than what job you have."

"Is there something specific you want to ask or are you just casually admonishing?"

"I'm casually wishing you well and I'm worried about your marriage."

"..."

"You think it doesn't show?"

"I've never thought at all about whether it shows."

"Be careful you don't mess up your life."

"Do you have more specific advice or are we staying on the general level?"

"I don't answer unasked questions. If you want to know, ask."

Her hand twitched, all the coffee spilled out onto the paper.

"I'm so sorry," she said, embarrassed.

"It'll dry, there's nothing to worry about."

"This time we don't have to make a stamp."

"Maybe this will be a new theme in our collection."

"It's gotten boring now, we'll have to think up something else."

Before the drawing dried, they had time to exchange another few lines.

"When did your hands start to shake?" he asked.

"In the orphanage, right before my mother came to get me. Hers didn't shake before the war, they only started after, so you could say at the same time as mine."

"And when did my hands start to shake?"

"When you finished elementary school."

"Why do I have it?"

"You don't ask why you've got your first gray hairs."

"Gray hairs don't get in the way of living."

"My mother's hands tremble, your mother's tremble, why shouldn't yours?"

"Will my children have it too?"

"We'll see," she said with a smile.

She didn't see.

Swiss Army Knife

He was on his way home from dropping his kids off at school, and heard the landline ringing while he was in the stairwell. His brief internal monologue went the same as usual: if it's something important, they'll call back—if it's nothing important, I'm not going to run up the stairs like a lunatic. Then he raced upstairs in fear, pulling the key out his pocket on the way.

"Grandma fell off a ladder, we have to go quickly!" So far no morning phone call had ever brought good news.

He hung up, dashed outside, and drove off to pick up his mother.

"She went up that little ladder that's always behind the living room door, she wanted to get Grandpa's summer jacket out of the wardrobe, she lost her balance and fell on her back."

"Did they call an ambulance?"

"No, Grandpa picked her up and drove her to the hospital."

"How could he pick her up if he isn't strong enough to lift a one-kilo bag of apples?"

"Don't get on my nerves! Somehow he picked her up and they went."

"I think he'd whine so much that she'd prefer to get up on her own to make sure he was all right. I hope they got there safe, I wouldn't get into a car with him, even if I had broken my back. Do you still drive with him?"

"What else am I supposed to do? I won't leave Mama alone."

"An ideal recipe for family suicide. I told all of mine they're not allowed near his car."

"Somehow I'm not able to do that."

"The stakes are pretty high, maybe it's worth it. Have you ever had an argument with him, a serious one?"

"Do you really think it's the best moment for this kind of chat?"

"We've got at least fifteen minutes until we arrive, we can spend it in silence."

"We've never had an open war."

"Do you like him?"

"Please, can we have this conversation another time?"

"I've had no contact with him."

"He used to bring you presents."

"And he always told me to promise I wouldn't break them. Once I refused to take something because I didn't want to swear the oath. Then he got offended and set Dad on me."

"And?"

"I didn't take the present, but I heard Dad say he understood, because I could even dismantle an iron ball."

"That was actually true."

"That wasn't actually a reason to blackmail a seven-year-old kid."

"Do you remember what the present was?"

"A 'Little Carpenter' set."

"Ahh, maybe you think you didn't take it, but you used the saw from that set to cut off the corner of my drawing board."

"When you were little, did he also make you swear you wouldn't ruin anything?"

"He had a different strategy, he'd get offended and then he wouldn't have to buy me anything anymore."

"So you did have run-ins after all."

"Never open ones. I'd do something different from how he'd planned, and he'd start sulking and stop talking to me."

"For a long time?"

"Until I made some kind of friendly gesture toward him. He liked it best when I apologized."

"I don't know who fell off that ladder, but Grandpa's car is parked in the trunk of a green Fiat."

"We'll deal with that later. Park and let's run."

• • •

His grandparents were waiting in the hallway. Grandma was in a wheelchair, and her hands on the armrests were shaking even more than usual. She was fresh out of testing; a slight concussion, two stitches on the back of her head, bruised elbows and back. Mom went to get the results and his uncle took the keys and ran to unpark Grandpa's car from somebody else's trunk. After an hour they left the hospital.

"Give me the keys, I'll drive you home," said Grandpa.

"We'll drive ourselves home afterwards. You guys get in, we'll go to your place first," replied the grandson with the firmest voice he could manage.

At the nearest intersection, they stopped to wait for a green light. When they were supposed to move, two cars approaching at high speed collided head-on right in front of their hood. A bang, flying pieces of chassis, smashed windows, and clouds of steam from damaged radiators. It all took no more than five seconds. The momentum swept both cars onto the sidewalk.

"Look, they just barely missed each other," said Grandpa spontaneously, with disarming bluntness.

The grandson looked at him in disbelief, then glanced in the mirror. Grandma was sitting unmoved, Mom was shaking her head and he could see her gathering herself to say something.

"All right, let's keep going," the grandson whispered,

more to himself than to them. "The situation here is clearly getting tense."

"Mama, I've moved all the summer stuff to the lower shelves. I'm begging you, don't get on that damn ladder again. I'll call in the afternoon and we'll figure out what you two need. We'll get going now."

"It's started," she said sadly, once they were out on the street. "Now it'll only get worse."

"We'll take that ladder away from them and it'll be okay."

"We're going to have to take away a lot more, and in the end, them themselves."

"What are we doing about the car? Grandpa made sure I gave him back the keys."

"Do you know how to immobilize it?"

"Without the keys I can't get to the engine."

"And without getting to the engine?"

Her son triumphantly took from his pocket a Swiss army knife Grandpa had given him many years before.

"What are you scheming?" asked his mother, surprised.

"Watch, keep out of the way, and be proud of me."

He was on his way home from dropping his kids off at school, and heard the landline ringing while he was in the stairwell. Something's happened to Grandma after all, he thought. He quickly mounted the last flight of stairs and picked up in time.

"Grandpa called. You'll never guess what's happened now."

"Tell me."

"Some anti-Semites punctured all four tires on his car."

Dress Rehearsal

It's hard to push a wheelchair over an uneven sidewalk. You have to be especially careful when you're on a family outing. It would be hugely embarrassing if something went wrong. Tipping over a wheelchair in front of your parents and children is more than an embarrassment, it would look like attempted murder. The slightest wobble and hunched-over Grandpa, along with his little blanket, would sail onto the cracked concrete flagstones.

He's rolling along like a king. His smartly dressed daughter pushes the wheelchair. The sidewalk is narrow, they walk single file. Behind the daughter is her gray-haired mother, behind her, the daughter's husband and the two grandchildren.

They've lined up behind me in a funeral procession, thinks the passenger in the wheelchair, they're doing a dress rehearsal. He can see they're upset, they want what's best, but when they look him in the eyes, they uneasily avert their gaze. He knows where they're headed, they've been talking about it for several weeks. That is, they've been talking, he's been listening. Since the stroke he doesn't speak, but he understands everything. He kept nodding. They thought he was agreeing, but he was just nodding. I knew you'd do this, he thought, I don't know myself how I'd behave if it fell to me to decide about one of you.

It's a family outing, except not all of them will return home.

His neck is bent, he can only look sideways or downward. He glances at his wife, who's walking on his comfortable side, so they can both see one another. She's loved, her gaze is serene, she's pretending everything will be all right. He looks at her and does his best to make sure his eyes aren't reproachful, but he's afraid that, despite his intentions, she might take it badly. He doesn't know what his face looks like now. Neurology can play tricks on your facial expressions, which is probably why they haven't let him look in a mirror since he got back from the hospital.

He'd like to see his daughter's face now. He's very curious what she's thinking. He'd like to know whether she mainly feels guilt or rather a sense of duty well fulfilled. He can't see his grandsons, but he can hear ineffectually muffled sadness. Just like at his own funeral. A man deserves to hear his eulogies while he's still alive. Maybe they'll come to a decision and everyone will say a few words, he thinks hopefully.

• • •

It's early fall, the sun is still giving off a faint heat. It's nice being outside. He's dressed in a dark coat that eagerly devours the warm rays. He hasn't worn it in a long time. It smells mainly like the wardrobe, but he can also catch a whiff of tobacco. He wonders if the pocket still holds the pipe he's hidden from his wife in recent years. He's curious whether he's the only one who associates autumn with the autumn of life. It sounds poetic, but that's it as far as poetry goes. That season is long behind him. For him, this autumn day is the final winter of his life, no doubt about it. He alone knows it, the rest of the procession is living in hope for the achievements of modern medicine. They're meant to be younger and smart, but what bozos they are. You're never going to see Grandpa on his feet again, he's never going to speak a word to you again, you dopes, he laughs at them in his soul.

The procession reaches the stairs up which, with the collective strength of the whole gathered family, they pull him into his new home. They inexpertly attempt to lift the wheelchair. Finally everyone other than his wife is bearing one-quarter of its mass. Good thing they're carrying me feetfirst, he thinks with a smile, at least it won't bring me bad luck. Out of breath, they place the wheelchair on the stone floor right by the reception desk. In their overzealousness they've carried him all the way through the lobby. When a person's worn out, they feel less guilty, he giggles mentally. He knows this isn't their first time here, but they're behaving as if they've taken him to explore new lands together. They look around with interest and praise the pretty sheer curtains and the glistening floor. Seems like they'd happily move in here themselves.

Grandfather casts a look at his wife and sees a beautiful older woman he's going to miss. He can tell she's sad. They've spent over fifty years together and spoken many times about what awaited them. It was clear to both of them that he—the more prone to illness—was the one who'd leave first. She had left, once. It took her a little while to understand what she missed was actually him. She came back. Now they don't know who's leaving who—whether it's him, leaving for the nursing home, or her, leaving him alone. He feels sorry for her, he wouldn't want to be in her shoes. She's the only one who knows his old body contains a young mind. She's wise, mature, lonely from now on, and soon to be a widow.

At reception—which really is an admission room—they've arranged matters quickly. The young ones stand facing the counter, placing the wheelchair so that Grandpa has a good view of the terrace. The last moment when the grown-up people—husband and wife—hold hands. They've held each other like this so often. They can feel what that clasp means this time.

The remaining formalities go smoothly. Elevator upstairs, room, bed. The funeral dress rehearsal has reached its end, he remarks in his head, the corpse is on the catafalque. Here's the remote for the bed, but best not to touch it, the nurse will come and set everything up the way it should be. We serve meals in the dining room downstairs, sir, someone will come get you in time, please don't worry. On Sundays we have concerts. You'll be happy.

He wasn't happy and he didn't know how to say so.

Reservation

You have to be lucky to catch them, and sometimes you succeed. There's this little café where they have their own table. You just have to pass the counter, go in almost all the way to the kitchen, then sit down in the nook with a pair of little two-person tables. You never know if both tables will be free or if people will come. But it's worth waiting, and sitting at one while you mark the other as reserved. You could use a newspaper, a jacket or a bag. While feigning a lack of interest, you have to stay alert. You need to hold the "reservation" until the moment they arrive together or—and this is an advanced-level task—when only one does. Recognizing someone on an online date seems tricky at first, but eventually doubt recedes and you can spot them from afar, as if they were holding a sign: "I've got a date here with someone I met online." This is the moment to make eye contact and obediently collect your things, freeing up the table. Something about that corner is tempting. Maybe it's the alcove promising intimacy, maybe the slightly low lighting that makes even the middle of a summer's day feel like late afternoon. They're drawn like moths to a flame. The spot has another advantage that date-goers don't realize: perfect acoustics. A person drinking coffee at the neighboring table can hear every word. They might even feel as though there's an amplification system in here. Suffice it to say that conversations recorded on a Dictaphone come out exquisitely.

This place is worth more than every single psychology department combined. Here you can observe life under laboratory conditions. A brave—or maybe it's better to say, experienced—researcher sits facing the test subjects, providing not only sound, but also a visual. Yet you must be very careful not to be noticed. The ironclad principles of scientific methodology dictate that you must not influence the test results.

There are days when—just like with fishing—you get nothing. No couples appear or, worse, the table gets taken over by some assertive customer. They pick up your reservation symbol and give a questioning look: "Whose jacket is this?" You have to free up the space and, concealing your disappointment, go on sipping your coffee. Read a newspaper, check your phone, but don't drop your guard, because who knows, maybe today you'll get to hear the most interesting story in your life. There are times when, after a long silence, you win the prize.

Rendezvous can be divided into genres, just like literature or movies. Slice-of-life, drama, extended interview, erotic, even science fiction. Comedies are the shortest and always take place at someone's expense; they last no longer than one coffee.

From the perspective of the neighboring table everything seems transparent. From this spot it's easy to see when someone's been miscast. If you'd had your own choice of actors, the action would be much faster paced.

The fifty-year-old woman who a moment ago was practically bored stiff drinking coffee with a slightly younger windbag, would be an ideal match for the guy from a week ago. He was fun and spoke openly about sex. They'd probably have hit it off quickly. Yesterday's backpacker had no chance of finding common ground with the blonde manicurist. He even looked embarrassed and kept glancing around, as if he was afraid someone he knew would spot him with her. He should have gotten the girl who fled the table when her date went to the bathroom. The charming man in his prime, instead of beguiling the free-spirited widow, should have met the lady who was at the same table not so long before. She was wearing a yellow wool suit—a skirt and jacket—and on her head, a matching pillbox hat. The experienced observer knows they'd have left together or at least made plans to meet again.

• • •

He's dying to butt in on the conversations. He could help the blind regain their sight. Give them a moment to chat, and then with a slight nod, invite them over to his table. Listen, it's not looking good, but here's a solution. For you, I'll find a knight, for you, a princess, and for you—whoever you like. It's not worth your time, torment, and frustration. I've been sitting here a long time and now I know well who'll make sparks with who. I've got this big sheet of paper with everything written out. Listen, let me help you, the sight of you all breaks my damn heart.

For years he's been sitting and eavesdropping on other people's lives. He rests from his own family and doesn't lose hope that he'll learn to be a partner someone can put up with.

Our Parents' Address Book

Once again we sit down by the phone and the two of us start calling—taking turns.

"Hello. I don't have good news, Dad's died."

"Sweetheart, I'm going to cry, I won't be able to talk."

"I just wanted you to know."

That's all I said over the phone, but I wanted to say much more. To thank her for getting my parents together. That was diplomacy of the highest order. She told Mom that Dad was interested in her, and Dad, that Mom was thinking about him. If not for her, we wouldn't exist in the world. And as a reward—at an interval of fifteen years—I phone with awful news. First, that Mom died in a car crash, and now, that Dad has died.

And I wish I could turn back time and not answer the phone when it rang early that November morning. I was still in bed. The call was from a number that didn't match my wife's or any of our children's. I wasn't burning to answer it, but it kept ringing mercilessly. It was an unfamiliar, international number. I turned my head away to get a little more sleep once the ringing went silent. It didn't. I answered and heard the voice of one of the closest people in the world to me, with awful news. I think of this friend like a sister, although we had different parents. We became siblings when years ago I dictated my mother's obituary to her over the phone. First my brother, my dad, and I wrote it together, then I called her, because I knew she wouldn't turn me down and would handle sending it to the newspaper. I dictated the contents, she repeated it like a cruel prayer—word for word—and so we became siblings to one another.

I picked up the phone on that November Sunday and became an orphan. My brother became an orphan a little later, because he's younger and I wanted him to go on longer having a dad. I dragged my feet until the moment I felt I was deceiving him.

He also found out from me that Mom had died, though that time I didn't manage to delay the news. When I answered that phone call, we were standing next to one another. My legs buckled under me and everything became clear.

Being the depositary for news of a person's death is very

hard. You can pass it on quickly, but unfortunately that doesn't make it disappear. Holding on to it for longer, even for a few minutes, gives the illusion of control, but condemns you to solitude. Better a sadness shared than the delusion of having the situation in hand on your own.

As I call, I find myself unable to avoid a short introduction. I say "hi," then I add that I don't have good news. I don't know how to get right to it. For the listener it probably doesn't matter; after all, it only takes a couple of extra seconds. So it only helps me, but I haven't figured out yet how to skip the preamble.

Time has passed, I call my brother. I say I don't have good news, but I don't think he guessed how bad it could be this time.

An hour later the two of us are calling our parents' close friends. We take turns calling; I go, he goes. We've worked out our own ritual. After Mom died it was the same. This way we both take care of one another.

He calls, we lock our teary eyes, he says into the receiver that our father has just died, and I feel like a viewer in a movie theater. Scripted lines fly by and don't always hit me. We divvy up our parents' friends fairly, none of the closest are spared from hearing the awful news directly from us.

I call—he looks me in the eye—and it occurs to us that we're the only two from our childhood home who remain.

"I don't have good news, Dad's died."
"..."
"Can you hear me?"
"Unfortunately I can."

"I don't have good news, Dad's died."
"I'll come right over."

"I don't have good news, Dad's died."
"I was afraid of this call. The last time you phoned I thought it was about this."
"That time it was okay, but not this time."

The two of us sit on the sofa—in front of us, a small rectangular table with our parents' open address book—we call. We have to call, because it's easier to say these things to someone else than to yourself. We call, we call, until—just like after Mom's death—we stop.

One more conversation will not give us our dad back. We're no longer afraid he might die, but we don't feel the relief of that fear lifting.

Now our phones begin to ring.

Our Father

Everyone thought it was overstimulation, because he was about to receive a distinguished professorship from the President of the Republic. He was sitting in his lab, then suddenly went pale and folded in half, as if made of modeling clay. His coworkers laid him on the floor and elevated his feet. After a moment he opened his eyes, looked around, and everything slowly returned to its place.

A few minutes earlier he'd been on the phone with his wife, who was talking about a visit from their older son. The one who for years had given them endless reasons to worry.

He was their family's first postwar child, a hope for a new beginning. Unfortunately from an early age he'd turned a razor-sharp tongue on them. He wasn't interested in school, the only reason he went was to see his friends. And he didn't hide it, he even seemed to take pride in it. In a family where everyone saw clearly that to be equal you had to be better, he grew up a dunce.

• • •

"You should be able to recite your multiplication tables from memory, even if you get woken up in the middle of the night."

"I'm supposed to recite multiplication tables," the rebel replied, "but you keep telling me if you get woken up at night you can recite the whole Our Father. So how about I learn the Our Father instead, if it's so useful?"

"Don't joke, that saved my life."

"And can multiplication tables save your life?"

He played hooky from his lessons, he didn't read books, he gave his parents sleepless nights.

"At worst he'll be a doctor like your father," his wife often said with a smile.

He worried about his son's poor grades and only relaxed after his high school finals. When the boy brought his diploma home, his father picked it up and held it out far enough that he could read the small print without glasses.

"Look Dad, I've got one B, just like you."

"I had all A's and one B in shop, that's why I didn't go to tech school. On yours I see all C's and one B in phys ed. Do you know what that means?"

"Yeah," replied his grinning son. "That my whole life I'm going to dig ditches."

"Why don't you tell us to what we owe this cheerful disposition of yours?" he asked, aggravated.

"To being lucky enough to get my high school diploma."

"I've had enough of this," he said, and left the kitchen.

He returned with the car keys, then opened the fridge and took a bottle of vodka out of the freezer.

"Now fuck off and I don't want to lay eyes on you for a week," he said, handing both items to his son.

It was the first time in his life he'd sworn at a loved one. He was ashamed of it, but years of built-up anger exploded in that sentence—in a way that surprised everyone.

"Was there any point getting so worked up?" asked Grandpa. "I kept saying he'd pass." He gave his grandson a hug and a little cash for the road. "You'll see, my grandson will become a doctor yet."

The boy didn't go into medicine, and everyone felt let down. He chose a different major, and everyone's hopes went up again. Everything started looking rosy, it seemed a long-awaited peace would finally settle over the family.

Before the professorship ceremony, he stopped by the institute for a moment. He sat down at his desk to look through the materials for his afternoon lecture with his fourth-years. As he was finishing, the phone rang.

"Have you got a moment?" asked his wife.

"A quick one, because I've got to go in a sec. Has something happened?"

She told him that their son had just left.

"He said he's been living with a woman for three months. I asked if he's happy, he said very. I was glad, because he, and we, deserve it by now."

"Do we know her?"

"No. I said I'm very glad he's happy. I also added that they shouldn't have a baby right away."

"That would be just what we needed!"

"And you know what he answered?"

"Oh no! Things were just calming down."

"He said they are going to have a baby."

"And what did you say back?"

"That I was very glad, and congratulations."

He hung up the phone and felt a wave of heat wash over him. He came to on the floor.

The three of them sat down together: he, his wife, and a friend who for a long time had counted as family. They waited for news from the hospital. They knew their son had gotten into the delivery room by pretending to be a medical student. They didn't completely understand why, but they did the best they could. Midway through the day they moved onto the balcony that overlooked the street. It was the start of winter, but feelings of expectation warmed them from the inside. They knew their son would come see them first. Although by four dusk had started falling, they didn't leave their observation post. A person who's waiting isn't guided by reason, but by the desire to shorten the waiting time, which is why the three of them stuck it out in the cold. By the time they spotted him, it was well after six.

He ran down the stairs three at a time. He knew he'd catch his son in the courtyard. He saw him emerging from around the building. He waited by the entrance to the stairwell and watched. He was trying to read his mood, but in the darkness he could only judge by the rhythm of his steps.

When the son saw his father was waiting for him, he sped up, then right away he started running. He ran into his open arms, hugged him, and started to cry. Harder and harder, louder and louder.

It was years since they'd been so close. The son held him in his embrace and squeezed hard. They stood like that for a few minutes, and his mother and aunt watched them through the open window two stories up.

"I've got a son," the son finally said to his father.

"You were crying so hard that I thought they were both dead."

"They're alive and well," he replied, laughing and wiping his eyes.

"Well then, did they let you go for a walk with your grandson?" asked his wife.

"They did, but after we got back our son threw a fit. I walked into the courtyard and he was standing at the window, shouting so the whole neighborhood could hear, that I'm not allowed to be late, he was scared to death that something had happened to us. I dashed up the stairs and he was waiting in the door, his eyes full of fury."

"To look after a baby you have to have at least a scrap of responsibility," said his son, looking him dead in the eye.

Transplant

"I'll wait for you at two o'clock in front of the bank," he said over the phone.

Except they both knew that two o'clock didn't mean two o'clock. They had a code no one else was able to use. Two always meant before two, just as three would mean before three, and quarter to five, before quarter to five.

At two in front of the bank meant you had to be early, so he didn't have to wait for you. In their temporal calculations the operative unit was the quarter-hour. The father set their meeting for two o'clock, meaning he would be there by a quarter to two at the latest. To avoid making him wait, the son arrived at one-thirty. His father was already there, because he didn't want his son to have to hang out in front of the door.

They greeted one another as usual—the son presented his head, and the father kissed it. That was how it had always been. He kissed the top of his head, smiled, and said he always

146

smelled the same. They went up to the bank doors, where the son let the father in first. Neither remembered when that custom had become a rule, but they both greatly valued it.

"Professor, I'm waiting for you gents over here!"

They entered the main room, his father glanced around and, slightly hunched, in an elegant tweed coat, with a brown leather briefcase in his hand, headed toward the clerk.

He used to feel a little embarrassed that anywhere his father had visited more than once, he was greeted with open arms. His father knew the latest from the lady at the post office, how her daughter who'd moved to the UK for work was doing, and who was looking after her grandkids. He'd talk to the mechanic at the car shop about his severely ill wife. One woman working at the grocery store always asked about his dad's health and said she'd never forget what he did for her. At a restaurant, first his father would inquire with the owner whether she'd managed to make peace with her neighbors, and only then place his order. And so on, everywhere he went to more than once. Remember, people behave like people when you treat them like people, he kept saying. He lived according to his own maxim; he left a trail of goodness behind him.

"How's your mom feeling, is she out of the hospital now?" he asked.

"Yes, thank you very much," the clerk replied, beaming. "We went to the doctor you recommended. He really helped, thank you."

"Glad to hear it!" replied the father.

He narrowed his eyes and raised his brows slightly. Making this little expression caused a respectable smile to appear on his face. It indicated satisfaction at a duty well performed, which was exactly how he imagined his social life.

"I've got all the paperwork together for you two. I'd ask the professor to sign first, in all the spaces I've marked."

The father opened the left flap of his jacket and took out a black Parker 51, the pen he'd been using for over forty years. He signed in all the indicated places and passed the papers to the clerk. After a moment, the form giving him joint control of his father's accounts lay in front of the son with spaces marked to sign.

"Could I please borrow a pen?"

"There are some papers you should sign with a fountain pen," said his father. "Take mine, and then we'll go buy you a proper writing instrument."

"I'll sign in ballpoint pen and then we'll go get lunch. I'll never be a professor, Dad. You've got to accept that," said the son, kissing his father on the forehead.

"I think I'm finally going to retire," said his father over lunch.

"I thought you were supposed to teach next year."

"I thought so too, but the situation is more than fluid. The department is moving into a new building, everything there is new."

"Have you lost the will to work or do you not like the new building?"

"I've never liked that building, but I've still got a little energy for work."

"And the will?"

"I've got that."

"But . . ."

"But they're not letting me take my desk with me, everything there is supposed to be new."

"Maybe there will be better desks."

"After my father died I took his desk to the institute, and I've been sitting at it for almost twenty years. I don't see why I should sit at a different one," said his father, annoyed.

"You're retiring because of a desk? Grandpa stopped working when he was almost ninety, you're only seventy-five."

"I'm not throwing that desk out."

"My desk's a piece of junk, maybe I could take it?"

"Do you want to?"

He did, and he brought it home.

His father moved into the new building and for two years he sat at a desk he never grew to like.

• • •

The first thing his son took out of his father's desk at home after he died was a small cardboard box. Its weight didn't surprise him, he knew what was inside. He knew, but he'd never seen the brass letters and numbers. He guessed he'd be able to use them to spell out his father's name, date of birth, and certainly that he was a professor. The question was, what else? Had he played roulette with time, did he bet on the date of his own death? He hadn't, he didn't—he was smart, and anyway he never threw money down the drain.

The father's son sat on the floor with his own son, both leaning on the desk. They took the letters out of the box; each was properly wrapped in a newspaper from when his mother's gravestone was made. It took five minutes to arrange them. Between the father's desk and the window—perfectly lit—lay his epitaph. All that was missing was the November date.

Sometime later he took out of the middle drawer a few Parkers and Sheaffers; his father's favorite Parker 51 wasn't there. He lay them out on his desk, which had once been his grandfather's desk. All of them black, some with silver caps, individual ones with gold elements. Design combined with physics, the best marriage, he thought, looking at the inherited set of noble writing instruments.

There are papers that should be signed with a fountain pen. That sentence now seemed less old-fashioned than when he'd heard it at the bank.

At the request of his father's second wife, he emptied his father's entire home desk and moved the items he'd taken out into his own. It was an odd transplant. While sitting at his grandfather's desk, he could smell his father's desk. One of the four drawers held pipes and the napkins on which many years ago they'd made imprints of coffee cups. They, in combination with the old files full of lecture notes, were what gave it the smell that inscribed itself forever in his memory as "Dad's desk."

Two years after his father died, he bought a Parker 51 and moved his father's home desk into his own apartment. Finally all the items had been returned to their own place.

His grandfather's desk awaits the next person to use it.

A Champagne Lament

He opened a bottle of champagne, thereby welcoming her into his club. Quietly and joylessly, more tender than enthusiastic.

A filter hung over her eyes, as if someone had perfectly calculated how much liquid was needed to blur an image while not allowing tears to flow. They had known one another more than half their lives, she didn't need a focused picture.

"Welcome to the orphans' club," he said quietly, not concealing his own emotion.

He poured champagne into the glasses and replaced the toast with an embrace. They sat down at the table and looked at one another. The silence that fell wasn't awkward.

"A beautiful funeral. Beautiful for being honest. Not a single false word about your mom. I think even she'd have been happy. Not too long, and above all not especially tearful. I liked how you also talked about her not being the nicest person in the world. About her determination and her battle to stay herself right until the end."

"It wasn't easy being her daughter, but I don't imagine I

was meant to talk at her funeral about someone she wasn't. She had no fondness for mothering, she didn't give me either the feeling of safety or of love that I needed, as any child does. But she was my mom, I didn't have any other. I don't know if it's easier to say goodbye to a caring parent or a callous one. I know that in the last days of her life I managed to do something for her; she died surrounded by concern and care in our home. And most importantly, she was willing to accept those from me. Without that I'd be having an even harder time now. She and I closed this chapter well. The rest I have to cope with myself. Is there any toast for these kinds of circumstances?"

"I think that would make the toast a lament," he almost whispered back.

"To our parents' memory, a champagne lament."

The champagne had gone tepid, so it suited the toast perfectly. They talked for a long time about parents. Some sick for years, others disappearing in the blink of an eye.

"It was touching to see you and your kids hug," he said, once they'd both set their glasses aside. "They were taking care of you."

"Yes, that sort of strange moment where the roles reverse."

"A nice one?"

"Yes, but I found it hard. Do you know how to accept concern and support from your own children? I remember after your dad died, your son didn't leave your side."

"It's a big barrier to overcome. It was a wonderful feeling, but it was weighed down with a sense of guilt."

"Guilt about what?"

"That it ought to be him getting support from me. It took me a while before I learned how to benefit from it. And then I did, but I worried about overdoing it."

"How could you overdo it?"

"By becoming someone who expects care. I have a radar for those sorts of situations. One of my kids says to the other, 'Go help Dad,' and I can immediately hear myself and my brother when we talked that way around our parents. A carbon copy. I know when we started talking that way. Where do you draw the line of what you're ready to accept from them?"

"I don't like that the line is moving. I'd really hate to lose control. The only way is not to live too long."

"How long is too long?"

His phone rings.

"Let me get this, it's my daughter," he says, and goes out into another room.

After a moment he comes back.

"She said she's in the area and she'd be glad to come pick me up. She doesn't want me to walk home, apparently it's gotten very cold and rainy."

Acknowledgments

To Junona Lamcha-Grynberg, Marcin Grynberg, Justyna Dąbrowska, Paweł Łoziński, Paweł Malko, Belka Otffinowska, Jacek Otffinowski, Alex Grynberg, Tosia Grynberg, Derda, Magda Kicińska, the Wisława Szymborska Foundation, Michał Rusinek, Paulina Małochleb, the Dom Źródeł Foundation, Dorota Pieńkos, Monika Jaromin, and Mariusz Pieńkos.

Some for support, others for creating the conditions for work, and some for both.

Thank you.

About the Author

Mikołaj Grynberg is a photographer, author, and trained psychologist. He is the author of *Survivors of the 20th Century, I Accuse Auschwitz, The Book of Exodus,* and *Jesus Died in Poland,* as well as *I'd Like to Say Sorry, but There's No One to Say Sorry To* (The New Press). *I'd Like to Say Sorry, but There's No One to Say Sorry To,* his first work of fiction, was a finalist for the Nike, Poland's top literary prize. He lives in Poland.

About the Translator

Sean Gasper Bye has translated work by some of Poland's leading writers, including Małgorzata Szejnert, Szczepan Twardoch, and Remigiusz Ryziński. He is a winner of the EBRD Literature Prize. He lives in Philadelphia.

Publishing in the
Public Interest

Thank you for reading this book published by The New Press; we hope you enjoyed it. New Press books and authors play a crucial role in sparking conversations about the key political and social issues of our day.

We hope that you will stay in touch with us. Here are a few ways to keep up to date with our books, events, and the issues we cover:

- Sign up at www.thenewpress.com/subscribe to receive updates on New Press authors and issues and to be notified about local events
- www.facebook.com/newpressbooks
- www.x.com/thenewpress
- www.instagram.com/thenewpress

Please consider buying New Press books not only for yourself, but also for friends and family and to donate to schools, libraries, community centers, prison libraries, and other organizations involved with the issues our authors write about.

The New Press is a 501(c)(3) nonprofit organization; if you wish to support our work with a tax-deductible gift please visit www.thenewpress.com/donate or use the QR code below.